The Apocalypse of Lloyd

Mike Sauve

MONTAG

First Montag Press E-Book and Paperback Original Edition October 2016

Montag Press
ISBN: 978-1-940233-39-0
Editor - Charlie Franco
Cover Illustrations and jacket © Phillip Nessen
Book design © 2016 Niall Gray
Managing Director — Charlie Franco

A Montag Press Book
www.montagpress.com
Montag Press
1066 47th Ave. Unit #9
Oakland CA 94601 USA

Montag Press, the burning book with the hatchet cover, the skewed word mark and the portrayal of the long-suffering fireman mascot are trademarks of Montag Press.

Printed & Digitally Originated in the United States of America
10 9 8 7 6 5 4 3 2 1

"I should not talk so much about myself if there were anybody else whom I knew as well. Unfortunately, I am confined to this theme by the narrowness of my experience."

— Henry David Thoreau – *Walden*

"Well I heard it advertised one day that the Bear Mountain picnic was coming my way."

— Bob Dylan – Talkin' Bear Mountain Picnic Massacre Blues

Part I

Preamble

For the prudish, for those easily shocked, for those with heart conditions, for those afeard of eternal damnation, proceed no further.

Foreword

Somebody once said, "A screaming comes across the sky," and it didn't seem to mean anything except it sounded cool. But then a screaming did come across the sky and it became clear that that guy knew something all along, starting such a giant book with that one line of terrible prophecy.

What follows is a chronological perspective of the shadows that fell across the world, across my hometown, across the love-of-my-life Monica, across the harlot sisters Emerald and Regan, across mom and dad, across poor Pierre the beagle, across the eunuch Scapino, across the many babes and old creeps in the L-S-C Community Theatre Workshop. The world's unraveling was a Stanley Kubrick production starring Dennis Hopper, strangely enough.

My own pre-Anger dysfunction became real adult dysfunction after I had a falling out with my lifelong friend and eventual Bund-leader Dan Good when we were 17.50, a few years previous to the events of this narrative. The falling out between D.G. and me is largely unrelated to the sixty days of worldwide Anger that preceded my descent into the hellmouth, but it is relevant as to why I was so needy and screwed up to begin with.

There is anger, Goddess, sing it, and of I, Lloyd, sort of son of Gary, sing of me too.

1
March 28

Even in end times I was stuck in my parents' basement. In Lac-Sainte-Catherine, Ontario, Canada. Near Lake Temagami. A burg. A place where all the video rental places had closed, but people still rented videos at gas stations, streaming never having caught on among our aging population.

There was a lot of pitchy discussion about how we should have gone to the mall to lay in 8-packs if not outright palettes of beans when the ugliness first reared on the 25th. We had four cans of Puritan brand stew; two bags of potatoes, soon to spore; a Coleman stove; a five gallon jug of water. We huddled around a scented candle because the electricity had been out for two days. My mom sat close to the candle so she could read. My dad was close to the candle so he could do a Sudoku puzzle.

Monica had promised to be here with me when we'd Skyped at the beginning. But she was not. She was not answering her phone, and I was leery of travelling the two blocks to her parents' house, due to the Anger-diseased citizens of L-S-C liable to harm me. Also, Monica's parents weren't fond of the age gap between us, though she had reached the legal age of emancipation, and nothing statutory was being perpetrated. The age of consent in Canada is 16.00. I was 19.75.

In the 19th century the term "outrage" was a euphemism for "rape." After Albert Fish was apprehended, he was adamant that he did not outrage his child victim Grace Budd even though he cut her into pieces and ate her. I was hoping Monica had not been outraged in either the antiquated or now-quite contemporary sense of the word. I also hoped she had not become Angry herself. Some can sublimate the anger disease, sexually that is, at least for a period, I'd read. Naturally I was willing to help her with that, as we'd already been dating for almost a month.

Cellular signals were still working at this time, so Twitter and Facebook were available on my phone. Fortunately I had two heavy duty external battery packs for playing Ingress. On the internet, a lot of jokes about the Anger disease accompanied the Angry comments. Even in end times, irony was the predominant mode of social media discourse. Eschatological irony turned out to be the richest irony of all. Many Tard the grumpy cat memes, believe that.

I learned that Bob Dylan had been killed in concert by a Bob Dylan enthusiast. I'd always planned to celebrate Bob's death with a bottle of Scotch and Facebook photos of me drinking the Scotch, and then maybe as the night wore on I'd record covers for a YouTube video, even though I am not a great singer. But we only had one bottle of whiskey, and my dad said we needed to save it as a both a possible disinfectant and as a possible accelerant. As an accelerant we could weaponize the whiskey. Pour the whiskey on a rag, create a bindle, wave the burning bindle at the Angry citizens of L-S-C when they encroached on our property type thing.

"Should we board up the windows?" my mom asked.

"Don't exactly have large enough boards for it," said Gary.

"Two doors nailed together?"

"Not altogether confident that would work."

Fire had consumed the town's lone mall, the Central Mall. Moot efforts to extinguish were made by the few remaining members of our volunteer fire department. Looting was then limited by the town's lack of a mall. So the smaller stores were looted until empty. Prescient owners of smaller stores had headed home with whatever supplies they could carry, push or drag. This was how it happened in L-S-C. Things were no doubt uglier in New York City or Cadillac, Michigan.

My dad feared it to be drinking water-related, so he had a touchy relationship with our stores of drinking water, but thirsty as he was, he had to take sips. He tried to compensate with a large Tupperware container out on the porch to catch rain. But who could say if the disease wasn't rained down from a malevolent God or some sky-Devil in the first place?

Less blue-eyed people were Angry than brown-eyed people, said reports. My eyes were blue. My mother's were blue. My father had black eyes because he was African-Canadian. I didn't know how black eyes ranked compared to brown eyes. My father was actually my step-father. But since he had been around since I was two years old I referred to him only as *Father*, or more commonly as *Dad*, or even more commonly by his name of Gary.

"Dad, what's the plan if someone breaks the window?"

"Shoot them."

"But then the window's broke and atmospheric poisons may leak in."

"Quit being a smartass."

2
Some Facebook and
Twitter highlights from March 29

Seriously, dudes on the street, I am not that hot, no need for all this…. #weird #creepy pic.twitter.com/sJ70kYU3Ns

Is the Brooklyn Nets game cancelled tonight? I have box seats! #Nets #RondaeHollisJefferson #AngerDisease?

I never realized there was this kind of porn on the Internet. #prolapse #forcedcuckold

> Reply: I could actually go for a forced cuckolding right about now.

> Reply: It's only fun if the cuckoldee is steamed about being cuckolded. It sucks when they're into it.

I wish I hadn't quit electric guitar. Now seems a great time to be tearing off a badass metal solo.

Green mist consumes Chicago.

Ray's Old Time Peach Farm rechristened Ray's Fuck Yard.

> Reply: Directions to Ray's Fuck Yard please?

Cool to shoot a person with the Anger disease zombie style?

> Reply: In self-defense, I say go for it, but if they are leaving you alone I guess the jury's still out.

Reply: Given current trends in the culture, the populous is pretty geared up for and almost enthusiastic about a zombie-like dehumanization of our fellow man and the 'go-ahead-and-shoot-your-fellow-man' privileges that go with it for remaining norms like us.

There's more to this than meets the eye.

Reply: Hands down the most obvious tweet of the year. Just perfect that in end times you are still the Internet's leading provider of worthless bromides.

Any idea where you can get those bath salts in Dearborne?

Receiving an unprecedented volume of OK Cupid messages.

Lo, the ghost of old Count Condu has come for us yet.

If my house had power I could have watched pornos and I wouldn't have done what I just did. #PowerForPornosPlease

Using a hay bailer to disembowel my brother's kids.

It's funny that Twitter is trending right now.

Who are all these new people on my Facebook friends list?

Reply: Images of corpses being uploaded as profile pictures on mine!

Reply: A lot of Dennis Hopper profile pictures too. And weird Dennis Hopper memes. Why?

Boy, have I had enough of this already.

"We chopped through the night, and we chopped through the dawn!" RIP Bob Dylan.

3

Monica hadn't responded to my twelve texts. I wasn't sure if I loved her, but I sure was fond of her. I hated to think of her suffering a Grace Budd-like fate. She'd never met my parents. She came over after they'd gone to sleep, for carnal purposes primarily, though we also always watched TV and smoked weed in the sub-basement.

My parents forbade me to leave, but I decided to make the trip if I didn't hear from her after a couple days. If I drove the CRV I didn't think much harm could befall me in such a short distance.

My dad had finished his Sudoku book, and, a bundle of nerves, was clicking a pen repeatedly.

"Can you stop clicking that pen so much?" I asked.

"That depends if you'll stop jogging your leg."

Pierre the Beagle did a little dance.

"The dog needs to pee," my mom said, "Put him on the leash. The last thing we need is for him to run away."

Out of some misplaced loyalty, the dog would not pee on the deck, so I took him to the backyard. Beneath the deck my neighbour Ken String laid in wait. He hissed at me and lunged. Pierre bit his neck. Mr. String was low to the ground so I stomped him, incapacitating him briefly. Pierre and I ran back inside.

"Did Pierre go pee?" my mom asked from the living room.

"No, I was attacked by Ken String."

Ken String punched his fist through our kitchen window. He was knocking away shards of glass with his bare forearm, cutting the hell out of himself. My dad remained calm, perhaps as a result of his military training. He picked up his .22 caliber rifle and shot Ken String directly in the temple. RIP Ken String.

"Geez. Sorry about that Ken," said Gary.

Ken String had been a good man, always willing to lend a hand when a deck or shed was being built. Now dead, by a gun that had last been fired in 1993 at a small rabbit.

"That window definitely needs to be boarded now," my mom said.

"Listen, I have no idea how to nail a board to a window," said my dad.

We were all thinking of that scene in *Night of the Living Dead* where they nailed boards to the windows, appearing to nail them beside the window, nicely covering them. That's what we ended up doing, but it wasn't easy and required 30+ nails and a solid hour of unscrewing the sub-basement door, and then me struggling to hold that door up while Gary nailed because I had limited nailing skills relative to Gary.

"What should we do with Ken String?" asked my mom.

"Leave him," said my dad.

"Then the Angry might know there are potential victims here," said my mom.

Gary looked annoyed, and said, "Let's shove him under the deck then," so we did that.

The dog whimpered because he still had to pee. I took him to the basement and tried to get him to pee on a newspaper like he'd done as a puppy. The dog wouldn't and so we

came back upstairs where he whined a while more and eventually peed on the living room carpet and looked ashamed about it.

My dad got out a bottle of Oxyclean and scrubbed at the pee, but because he didn't want to waste water he just ground the Oxyclean into the pee and made a bigger mess.

4

I received an email from my boss at OmniVoice Communications, a call centre located in a former tire plant in the town's second emptiest industrial park. When the tire and steel work moved to various BRIC nations, and the population of L-S-C grew underemployed, the call centres came in with their minimum wage three-month contracts and their basic call-centre bullshit that anyone who's ever worked at a call centre won't require a detailed description of.

Dear Employees,

Over the past 18 months, our TEAM at OmniVoice has offered Customer Service Solutions to satisfied clients ranging from The Toronto Star to Bombardier and on and on. We truly realize that outsourcing contact with customers is no easy decision for a reputable company like Bombardier, and so we aim for Bombardier Level Professionalism at all times.

As you know, our regional metrics for first-call resolution resolutions were sterling, way above par.

That's because the people of Lac-Sainte-Catherine have an old-fashioned work ethic, and do not become cynical when faced with the sometimes psychologically-draining world of call centre work.

Our Goals were consistently met and sometimes exceeded. Much of this I attribute to the movie pass program.

That level of professionalism has now been called into question as a result of Saturday's cannibalism episode at the work site. Rest assured, we are focused on renewing our reputation once this unfortunate period passes. Certainly, we won't be the only organization that suffers a hit to our reputation. I just read that the CEO of ComWave cut off his son's penis, diced it up, and put it in a poutine, with penis chunks in lieu of cheese curds, and then ate the poutine, and moreover he did this in a video blog that was sent to all of ComWave's top clients. I'm thinking these clients would prefer a single incident of cannibalism by a cadre of rogue and disgruntled employees vs. a penis-chopping and penis-Poutine-eating from the very CEO of ComWave.

Because we cannot maintain our Best Practices during this time of strife and unrest, we have shuttered our doors for the time being. Needless to say this comes as a blow not only to our clients who depend on our customer service acumen to grow their business, but also to you, the employee, expecting and entitled to a paycheque.

Should banking resume I can send you all E-transfers for the two weeks owing. There will be no pay

issued for the 24th, because as you know, you were sent home early at 10:15. Since that was only 15 minutes of active work time I have decided it's easier to round down to 0 work hours for that day.

Also, if we do not resume business, chances are you will not receive your yearly CSR bonus or any percentage of it even if you were on pace to earn it because if we do not resume business the fiscal year will not have reached its conclusion.

Best regards,
Andrew McCarrick

PS: A desire I once thought bad has overwhelmed me. Does anyone remember Davey? That fifteen-year-old kid who dropped out of high school and then joined the team at OmniVoice and then got fired for smoking pot in the handicap washroom? Well, that guy wasn't castrated or anything, but let's say I had cause to reexamine some of my priorities in the wake of Thursday's early-morning cannibalism fiasco, and now Davey and I are exploring some feelings that, previous to the outbreak, were so far suppressed as to have been non-recognizable. Yes, it's been a real bone-fest over here at the McCarrick home, with Davey and me. I wanted to share with all of my trusted employees that Davey and I plan to elope if this horror ever ends. And if the horror does not end, I'll still be grateful for these fine hours spent in Davey's downy and new chest hair.

We accomplished some great things at OmniVoice Communications, some really first-rate Customer Service and some serious ROI for our clients, and

God-willing we will one day accomplish those things again.

I had experienced nothing all that great at OmniVoice communications, although the cannibalization of Blind Harv (not actually blind) the day manager was a site to behold. I only saw Blind Harv's cannibalization in its early stages, choosing to run out the emergency exit as soon as more than one person got in on consuming Blind Harv.

I wasn't sure Andrew McCarrick's desires were ever all that suppressed. He was always big on giving these neck-rubs, occasionally to females but mostly to males. We'd freeze up in terror when suddenly feeling his hands on our necks. With guys he'd always ask some question about sports or hunting or an action movie then in theatres, so the neck-rub victim could observe quite demonstrably the repression of his personal gay desire for you, the brawny- or-else-narrow-necked-male adolescent or otherwise early-20s male. I didn't begrudge him shacking up with Davey because last I heard Davey had been living in a shanty in Morningside Park, so more power to Davey for working this angle, I figured. And more power to A. McCarrick for only fornicating with a youthful and impressionable Davey rather than being out outright murdering and castrating and etc.

But then I read a Tweet from a co-worker that said Davey was nailed to a crucifix on Andrew McCarrick's lawn at that very moment. This led me to wonder if Andrew McCarrick was crazy the whole time he was describing penis poutines in that ROI email or if the email was legit and McCarrick had lost his marbles only afterward and then started nailing up Davey.

And the movie pass program was a giant scam.

5

Perhaps a macro approach would benefit the narrative. Well, because L-S-C is where I was born and raised, and where all my experiences are derived from—where I'd spent all my happy childhood nights, often alone, pining for various girls, eating chicken wings at least twice a week. L-S-C was where I was taught to drive by Gary, broke down crying way too often as an early adolescent to ever be trusted by the upper caste of popular hockey players, where I'd hoped and sometimes prayed—because of all that this document is primarily interested in the inseparable intersection of my own micro-level life and the fallout of the Anger disease. But I believe that my own L-S-C experience can be unpacked and extrapolated to the world level, like one piece of a RAR contains all the information of a larger archive, and simply by plunking that one piece into WinZip the thing emerges whole. The breakdown was systemic, rules broken and resources plundered. Loved ones eviscerated, boiled, baked, sautéed, you name it—component parts broken down in any number of ways.

I pictured Monica leaning her head back and laughing her slightly grating laugh. I thought of her ripped jeans and the red hoodie that she wore almost every day, and how that hoodie framed her figure so effectively. I wondered what kind of Monica existed now. Was she angry? Fallen victim to an Angry party? Suddenly into forced cuckolding but not necessarily forced cuckolding of a violent nature? I had to cherry-pick the most positive thoughts from the most bleak to create within myself a system of emotional control. I had to become one of Kaczynski's "Cool-headed logicians."

I had only heard the phrase "Cool-headed logicians" once, in an A & E Biography of Ted Kaczynski, and while

I did not usually go around aspiring to be a cool-headed logician, I feared that these external thoughts might be the advanced guard of coming insanity.

When my parents fell asleep I took the car keys to the CRV and left for Monica's house.

6

I had met Monica at a party at Rob Calcofluco's. Young people start drinking early in L-S-C. At 13 our parties had the type of enthusiasm usually associated with frosh events. By 19 and 20 we partied in the staid fashion of retirees, sipping rum and cokes, making elaborate Caesars with salt rims and celery garnishes. I'd lost my real friends years previous and only came out with Calcofluco's cretins when I couldn't bare another night alone in my parents' home. Too much of the prime of my life had been spent on 4chan reading implausible creepypastas, looking at images of gore for no reason, watching the vilest of vile pornography just to face the loneliness of my world in the morning.

Rob's younger brother was hosting his own party downstairs featuring attractive high school girls. Tongues clicked as I left the kitchen scene for the younger one. I asked a pretty girl named Sarah for a beer to strike up a conversation.

Moments later I broke up a fight between an underclassmen bully and his victim by holding the aggressor in a full-nelson. It's hard to get out of a well-applied full nelson regardless of how ripped you might be, especially if you haven't finished growing. My policy was to always break up

fights via full-nelson when girls were around because it gives you all the esteem of a fight victory with far less personal danger, plus some air of pacifism that girls seem to admire.

Afterwards, Sarah's friend Monica, who'd seen me at a previous Calcofluco function, started a conversation with me. During which I requested and received the contact info of both girls. At home I found Monica and Sarah on Facebook, downloaded their photos, uploaded the photos to 4chan's request page and requested someone skilled in Photoshop make fake nude X-ray photos out of them, as I did after meeting any attractive female.

Two nights later I asked both Sarah and Monica to meet me in a nearby park to hang out. Sarah declined, but Monica accepted. She had a bad outbreak of acne and teeth that weren't perfectly straight, but still nice in their own way. I'd had acne and my skin had only recently cleared. I felt hips as I pushed her on the swing. I noticed her sized-four feet dragging through damp bark chips. I kicked some snow around, inhaled the -13.875 Celsius night. We returned to my parents' house and snuck downstairs, electrons and ions exploding and charging the air between us. Despite having had a few willing parties come down into the sub-basement over the years, sex had always been something I watched on the Internet and nothing more. My IRL sex efforts always resulted in an unpleasant and ineffective jamming, I guess due to my general selfishness as an aspirant love-maker. Though Monica knew what she was doing, panic still got the best of me. Sad that I was the one nervous one when she was in the middle of adolescence, and I I guess an adult, attending an institution anyway and meeting customer service metrics like it wasn't a thang.

The next time it worked, my only perception being, "It is happening!" with an underwriting sensation of, "Do not stop thrusting lest you lose momentum." Anyway, was able to thrust until official. The next night I was more confident

and it was like the sex in movies where everyone has a religious experience. That's how it had gone every night since late January. We'd smoke pot, have religious experience sex, and listen to *The Wall* Disc 2 over and over again to my parents' chagrin. I hate to overemphasize our sexual congress in a crass way, though it was undeniably a big deal for me, and way better than scrolling listlessly through the poison pages of 4chan each night. What felt best was having that little friend to go to L-S-C's under-patronized nature spots with, to scold as she played Frisbee at a skill-level beneath my Frisbee standards, to talk to.

Since I had ostracized myself from Dan Good et al at the end of high school, it had been some time since anyone other than my mother had laughed at my jokes. We did not laugh much at the call centre; such was the stifling nature of the call-centre environment. The classes I'd attended at the L-S-C Community College were attended predominantly by older and desperate second-career sorts, meaning no congenial atmosphere of youthful good times like you might see on college campuses or movies about college campuses. What a fine month it was with Monica. And why just moments before an Anger disease?

7

Weeks of waiting for my parents to retire so Monica and I could indulge our desires had finely-tuned my ear to the sounds my parents made preceding their nightly voyage to the sleepy-town. The running of the tap for tooth-brushing

was foregone due to our only water being in a five gallon container, but I heard the floorboards before their box spring creak and the louder creak of the mattress itself. Despite their warnings that I was not to leave, the keys still hung on the key-rack. I'd been sneaking out of the house late at night for years, rolling the Honda CRV out of the driveway in neutral, only igniting the engine once on the street.

The first thing I noticed was my dear old neighbor Ms. Robertson fileting her beloved cat Michel. The word *fileting* is appropriate because she was holding up thin butcher-like cuts of cat meat, holding them above her maw like a crab-meat enthusiast might hold a chunk of crab meat above their maw. She then dropped the raw cat filets in and slurped them on down. I waved. She waved back.

Our other neighbour Mrs. Desbiens was vigorously pleasuring herself in a negligee that brought to mind the negligee Nicole Kidman wore in the film *Eyes Wide Shut*. This might have elicited some lust in me, Mrs. Desbiens being a both comely and busty older woman, but the tongues she spoke in were a big turn off. I waved. She ran at the SUV and wiped what I presumed to be woman jizzom on the passenger side window. I ignited the ignition and closed the sunroof.

I spotted a group of young Chinese people huddled behind the Skrellman family's Hydrangeas. The apparent leader was saying, "You know its first order so you can get this rate equation, and this part is the slope. From the graph you have, the slope = 0.434 k. Because it's locked, if you plot your line, and account for the natural lock, then the slope = k. That's where the 0.434 k comes in. If you lock the exponential, is that clear? Then you can solve for K because you can get slope."

This seemed an aberration to me. First, because racial diversity in L-S-C is almost non-existent. It's 47.5%

French-Canadian, 47.5% Italian-Canadian and the remaining 5% skewed heavily towards Irish, English, and various Nordic. Asians, Africans and Hispanics were in the 99th percentile. My dad's own blackness turned the occasional head, even in that year of grace 2014. And second, why some engineering or diffusion/kinetics tete-a-tete on the riotous streets of L-S-C post-midnight? And where did the suddenly influx of Asians come from? Certainly they didn't attend the college. The local community college had no programs of study resembling engineering or hard science of any kind. The college's courses skewed towards low-end social sciences and practical programs like Office Admin, which really meant, "How to be a secretary."

"Where did you guys come from?" I yelled out the window.

"Where did you come from?" the apparent leader asked me.

"My house, right over there."

"We too came from our houses."

"You don't live around here."

A couple of them shrugged.

The route to Monica's required only two quick turns: off my street onto Bell Drive, and from Bell Drive onto Spring Avenue, but Bell Drive seemed to end in a dead end that night, representing the first reality glitch that I would experience personally, but even with Spring avenue no longer existing I found myself turning into Monica's driveway.

I considered knocking. The door was locked, but the window above the back-porch wasn't. I squeezed through. Inside, her step-father was passed out drunk on the floor, clutching a bowie knife. He woke and brandished in my direction. I put a hole in his guts with the 22. He screamed

and moaned until I put a hole in his head, blew up half his head more like.

"I hath killed," I thought, feeling the situation warranted a little olde English. I considered rubbing his blood onto my face in a way that would evoke Marty Sheen's anguish at the beginning of *Apocalypse Now* but then thought better of it.

I did feel a little remorse. Part of it was desensitization from gore sites such as r/watchpeopledie, but also Monica had told me of his insidious emotional abuse. Not abusive enough for Children's Aid to intervene, but abusive enough to corrode a young woman's self-worth. Plus we were in an Anger disease/anything-goes scenario, so rationale was not hard to come by. Anyway that was the Lloyd-man's first kill.

"Hello?" Monica yelled.

"Monica?"

"Oh thank God."

"It's me."

"I know."

"Where are you?"

"Locked in this trunk!"

She was indeed locked in a big royal blue trunk. Once it was unlocked she emerged naked and reddened.

"How did you get in there?"

"He said he was saving me for later."

She vomited and then dry-heaved for a couple minutes. I had this absurd idea to find some paper towels to wipe up the vomit.

"What did he do?"

"Weird stuff. I don't want to talk about it."

"Where's your mom?"

"At a conference in Brampton."

"Is she alright?"

"I don't know I've just been released from this ding-dang trunk," she said as she worked out the cramps contracted from her trunk-confinement. I felt shameful for admiring her nude bod given the circumstances, yet still I admired.

"Come on. We should get out of here. Let's go back to my house."

"Let me get something to drink first." She drank two glasses of water from a Brita filtered jug in the non-functioning fridge, and then ate three pickles.

"Pickle?" she asked offering the open jar. Then she laughed at the bizarre contrast of pickles v. the recent murder of her step-dad + the whole brains on the wall scene.

"Let's gather the canned goods," I said.

Bell Drive was back to normal on our return to the MacDonald household. The engineers were no longer convened. Though Mrs. Robertson was still out, the cat had been flung aside and now she was clipping her toe-nails with a feverish enthusiasm, nail clippings boomeranging through the air in front of her. She again waved.

Easing the door shut, I nodded at Monica = 'Things will be alright, maybe.' Pierre didn't bark because he could sense me, even from my parents' bed, where he lay. I placed blankets over the hard basement floor and made love to Monica with a desperation borne on her end out of being trapped in a trunk and borne on mine out of fear I'd never touch her again. We crept to my bedroom and slept in each other's arms. I had spent years on that bed cuddling a pillow, generating sufficient pelvic warmth to imagine it as a female companion. Nothing more depressing than meeting your pulsing desires with a sack of cotton and foam.

The rising sun returned. It became apparent that there'd been no reason to sneak into the room. The showdown with my parents was inevitable. Still, probably

more tactful not to have woken them in the dead of night, we agreed.

"Go out first and tell them I'm here," Monica said.

"Let's go down together. There's solidarity in that."

She brushed her hair with my hairbrush, and put her red hoodie over her tank-top. How I'd come to love a tank-top. I'd always been enthusiastic about tank-tops, but this was the tank-top of someone who was mine.

My mom was boiling water on the Coleman stove for tea. This struck me as an egregious abuse of our Coleman gas, but one of the issues never broached in our household, or any households in L-S-C that I knew of, was caffeine dependence.

"It's nice to finally meet you," said my mom without turning, strata upon strata of passive aggression crepitating and popping.

"Likewise," Monica said demurely, and then the power came on, for pornos, ostensibly, were the porno-requesting Tweets to be believed. With it came the water. Gary had explained to me that after a short period of time water pressure required electricity.

"I'll start boiling potatoes!" Gary screamed.

8

While my laptop booted in the basement I plugged in my many devices to charge. Upstairs, my parents boiled and broiled while watching the kitchen television. None of the news stations broadcasted, and all Gary could find were reruns of *Cake Enthusiast* and *Half-Ton Mistress* on TLC, the

so-called Learning Channel, programmed by an autonomous machine months ago.

Monica hadn't brought any of her devices and asked if she could use mine. I experienced chagrin at the invasion of my digital privacy, but I couldn't really say no. Monica checked email and found one from her mom, with the standard, "Be careful, be safe, we'll both make it through this and everything will be fine," but it was three days old, so who could guess what had happened since. The rest of her emails were DealGetters deals that weren't even applicable in crappy old L-S-C but only in Toronto, where Monica had visited once and aspired to visit again.

I hadn't been checking Facebook as often as Twitter and email. So only then did I see a FB wall post from Regan Jefferson, subjectively speaking maybe the prettiest girl in my grade at St. Michael's Collegiate. She had sat beside me in about 30% of my classes, exploiting my smarts during many group projects we completed together. She'd even come to my house once, the basic deal being, "You help me with do my Calculus = You get to be in my presence." I had gratefully accepted this deal, even boasting of it to Dan Good at the time.

Years removed from the last time I'd seen her at graduation, I still thought of her regularly. Because of her elite social status, and my role as something of a sardonic or cruel clown, she never could have been mine. I often fantasized of a world population shortage scenario that forced carnality and procreation upon Regan and me. During a brief period in grade eleven we spoke on the phone nightly, leading me to believe I had some outside chance. I told a few putative friends of this perceived chance. When she then sat beside me at an assembly it set the L-S-C Twitter-verse a-buzz with gossip. Regan + Lloyd etc., all very sarcastic because she

was royalty and I the sardonic clown figure, and also named Lloyd, which had never been to my advantage. She'd tactfully disregarded the rumours, but must have realized they'd started with my naïve hopes. Then one phone conversation had gone like this:

Regan: "Boys are so mean. I'm so sick of them."

Lloyd: "You don't think I'm mean, do you?"

Regan: "I'm talking about boys I would want to date."

That simply—my ineligibility was stated plain.

After that conversation the fantasies took on a vengeful tone that I will not convey in detail because I consider myself a feminist and am ashamed of having had hateful revenge sex fantasies about a person who, despite the above descriptions of homework exploitation, had always been kind to me, and in one of those perversities of high school life—a friend.

Her status read: "Anyone who wants to come use my body is welcome to. There are guards at the entrance. Five minutes per person. You will be frisked upon entry so no weapons. Enter the driveway with your hands up or you will be shot. Please RSVP to my inbox or inquire about busy/light periods of the day."

Her parents were rich and the property was more like a compound. I wondered who the guards were. I hoped her brothers weren't a party to this. Had the whole Jefferson family's Anger manifested in this one collective fetish? I'd always wondered if being a brother to such a desirable human being might not be torturous. Maybe these were the brothers' long-standing latent desires laid bare: to stand guard over a big line of guys waiting for a five-minute roll in the hay with old Regan. Or more likely it was a trap.

"What are you looking at?" Monica asked.

"Hilarious George Takei status," I said, "Man, you cannot keep that guy down."

9

The smell of frying bacon nearly made me forget the ongoing Anger. We had stored our limited proteins in a cooler when the power first went out. Since the power could go back out at any time, now was the time to do some some cooking. I made a hilarious bacon/end times meme on MemeGenerator, but no one on Facebook liked it.

Monica and I watched a segment of *Wife Swap*. As the swap ramped up, an image of a bloody Dennis Hopper head on a stick was superimposed over one of the dissatisfied spouses. This meant the TV shows were not machine-programmed months ago after all. The TV shows were something sinister. Who'd have thought *Wife Swap* could get any more sinister?

"Chow time," my dad hollered. He was always employing *Charles in Charge*-era clichés like this. I rolled my eyes at Monica. She didn't understand the eye roll, not having accumulated as much bile related to Gary's cliché abuse, and became defensive because she thought the eye-roll was directed at her for some mystery offense.

"Dennis Hopper eh?" I said.

"Who's that?" asked Monica.

"Director of *Easy Rider.*"

"Oh ya?"

"Bad guy in *Speed.*"

"Oh, right. From back in the day."

These were the problems in dating an individual who'd only been on the planet for 16.59 years; then again, most rubes my own age in L-S-C wouldn't have known Dennis Hopper from Bob Hoskins anyway.

"Chow time," my dad repeated, louder.

Upstairs, the first thing my mom asked was, "So, did you two meet at the college?"

"I'm in high school," said Monica.

My mother blinked about 38 times in less than ten seconds. She was overeducated for our town, having received not one but two terminal degrees in fields in limited demand in our cultural backwater or anywhere really. Fields so esoteric that she had to travel to conferences in other nations if she wanted informed discussion. One of her PhDs dealt with the paintings and writings of William Blake, inter-textually, the paintings and writings combined or something, and the other terminal degree was also intertextual, about the paintings of William Blake v. the verse of Milton. For many years now she had the de-rigueur bright red hair of her type that she dyed each month. She wore jet-black turtlenecks and big round green framed glasses, the kind that you just didn't see in a place like L-S-C. Her marriage was one of two interracial marriages in the whole town. The other interracial couple often waved when we saw them out for their punishing marathon-length runs. There may have been other interracial couples, but if so we'd never encountered them.

My dad took four strips of bacon. I took four strips of bacon. My mom took two strips of bacon. Monica took three strips of bacon. One strip of bacon remained.

I took a rather large portion of potatoes. My mom took a portion half the size of my portion. My dad took a portion 2/5ths larger than mine. Monica took no potatoes, as only three cubes remained after my dad's aggressive potato grab.

"Did you see anything weird on TV?" I asked my parents.

"Dennis Hopper," said my mom.

"You think Dennis Hopper is somehow behind all this?" asked Gary.

"I could hardly imagine why. I think it's a general

breakdown in logic and order," said my mom. "So, Monica, you walked over here in the night, or what?"

"No, I was rescued by Lloyd. I'd been locked in a trunk."

"How horrible," my mom said, "By whom?"

"My step-dad."

"I shot and killed him," I said.

"Lloyd!"

"What? Dad killed Ken String."

"My son, a murderer," she said with an ugly mix of woe and irony.

"Mom these are zombie-like conditions. It doesn't count as old-fashioned murder anymore."

"Yeah, and by day two in that trunk I was wishing all sorts of bad things on Dave," said Monica, "We weren't that close. He'd only been living with us for a year and he wasn't nice to me, but ya, still, I know my mom will be upset. She's in Brampton right now, so I'm really sad about that."

"Those canned goods by the door are from Monica's house," I said, wanting to show that she had contributed to our whole setup, and that she wasn't just freeloading on our eggs, bacon and bread.

We each had one egg, which seemed kind of stupid and hilarious, I thought, somehow. You never saw one fried egg on a breakfast plate.

Pierre the dog sat on the floor hoping food would fall. Ordinarily I snuck him things, as that's what I'd want someone to do for me were I a dog, but given our rations and Monica not even getting potatoes I decided each calorie needed to go in my stomach.

My dad patted his stomach. Four potato cubes remained on his plate. He put these back on the original potato plate, or on the greasy paper towel that covered it anyway.

"Monica, you didn't get any potatoes," he said

"Oh, thanks," she said, as she pushed the potatoes onto her plate, and squirted ketchup.

"Pass the salt," she asked my mom, and after two beats of no salt forthcoming, added a very polite, "Please," and then, as the salt was on its way, an unnecessary, "Ma'am," which betrayed her discomfort, but at least she was trying.

My dad chinned air at me, "Did her step-father put up much of a fight?"

"Gary!" my mom said = 'Let's not discuss grisly details of Monica's step-father's recent death at the hand of our son.'

"No," I said, "Waved a knife at me and under the circumstances I believe that justified shooting."

Now I gave Pierre one potato cube under the table. My dad asked if anyone wanted the last strip of bacon. I said that I did. He split it in half and gave me half.

10

My dad asked me to help him in the sub-basement. It was the same depth as the entire basement, but part was carpeted and part was not, and the non-carpeted part we called the sub-basement, again, despite the exact same elevation.

We inventoried various sharp-edged items like screwdrivers, hacksaws, and paint scrapers before constructing makeshift weapons like the classic nail nailed through a board for like an eye-destroying nail-board weapon.

"Let's line these up by the door so we can defend ourselves in case of full-scale attack," he said.

"Hmm, in case of full-scale attack, maybe it's best not to have this big weapons cache visible for our enemies to use against us once they've overtaken us," I said.

Despite his military experience and my almost total lack of world experience, my dad had always respected my intellect, as my IQ was 146.749 and his was only 123.245, according to an online test we'd taken once. He ran the blade of a hacksaw gently against his palm to gauge its sharpness. He frowned, either at the dullness of the hacksaw or at my shitting all over his weapons placement strategy.

"What if the Angry person is one of us?" asked Gary.

"Subdue them."

"That won't be pleasant," my dad said, "Your mother won't want to be subdued."

"You may be the hardest to subdue," I said, my dad weighing just upwards of 225.85 pounds and in excellent shape for a 58.55-year-old man.

"Let's make a pact," he said, "If I sense it coming on, I'll confess at the onset and willingly submit to confinement."

"Until when?"

"Don't know. A cure, something."

"So we confine you for weeks or months on end, tending to you with sips of water and cubes of potatoes for as long as the potato supply lasts?"

He raised his palms.

I considered telling him about the external thoughts I'd experienced—the frequent recurrence of the phrase, "Cool-headed logicians" or the sighting of the anomalous Chinese engineering team that hadn't seemed real. Were these signs that I too was now infected, or were they merely new rips and tears in a world coming apart at the seams?

As I was about to, he said, "Do me one favour Lloyd? Quit it with the goddamn Pink Floyd."

I must have looked pretty horrified because Gary patted me on the shoulder before continuing, "That was phrased bad. But my suggestion is that you choose some other music. That album has always been special to your mother. You probably recall it from your childhood. Maybe that's why it holds emotional value for you. If you think about that, it's weird. You should not be getting your infancy all mixed up with your sex life. Either way it's creeping your mom out in a serious way. She doesn't want to be the type of mother who begrudges her young adult son a healthy sexual blossoming at a more-than-appropriate age..."

My face reddened. I knew full well my 'blossoming' (gross choice of words!) was several years overdue by L-S-C standards.

"...or discuss or think about your blossoming, but what we both want is some different music covering up those sounds. Sounds, by the way, that can be heard quite clearly through the floors. This is an old house."

"First, quit using the word blossoming so much. Second, okay."

"That would be an enormous relief to me. I'm glad that we could talk about this."

We shook hands, as if in agreement.

11

My parents read in the living room while Monica and I stuck to the basement TV. We only saw one more Dennis Hopper-head impaled on a spike. A teaser for a Geraldo Rive-

ra interview with Charlie Manson aired unexpectedly, and while out of place during a commercial break of *The Montel Williams Show*, at least it was a previously existing clip and not newly minted in some reality studio of occult origin. Its airing may have been occult, but its production was not. The occult production of the Dennis Hopper image disturbed me most. It was the old Ameriprise pitchman Dennis Hopper's head on a pike. Who or what was producing and televising this stuff? I imagined data towers at TBS Superstation world headquarters, glowing a malevolent red, run amok, no longer responding to protocols.

Later Monica and I played cribbage. Good afternoon fun, because, as mentioned, we hadn't spent many afternoons together in the month previous, just sneaking off to filthy teen enclaves together or else sharing the wee hours in a lover's embrace. I beat her handily. I'd had to teach her how to play and she played poorly, often missing out on 15s. At first this was forgiven, but excessive forgiveness is no way to teach, so after three hands I enforced the letter of the law and rightfully claimed any and all missing points in her hand as mine. As a result, I came within a few points of skunking her.

"Want to play again?" I asked.

"No thanks," she said.

We then had a nice roast for dinner. This time there was enough to go around. Mrs. Robertson was visible from the kitchen window, doing pushups on her lawn, the frilled tips of her nightie softly kissing the grass with each down stroke. We all hoped she wasn't planning an attack against us. When she saw me in the window she waved. I waved back. My mom rebuked me, saying that even a wave might encourage her to storm our grounds.

At 8 pm the power went out again. Panic ensued because we'd been so busy playing cards and living relatively

large under the circumstances that we had failed to take adequate measures against the next outage. We hadn't made enough ice, and now badly needed ice to refill our cooler. Ice-making should have been a top priority, but this was neglected in favour of celebratory bacon and roasts. There were some bass-heavy accusations on my part regarding ice until my parents turned it on me = 'If you're so smart why didn't you make ice then?' which was true, my only argument being that they as parents were historically responsible for the preservation of our proteins.

Fortunately the power came back on after a half hour. My mom made a big show of filling the ice trays = 'A woman's work is never done,' with a lot of haughty sub-breath commentary.

My parents usually went to their bedroom around 10:30 and turned off the lights between 11 and 11:30. On this night it was excruciating as the lights in their room stayed on until almost midnight. Monica and I smoked weed as we waited in the sub-basement. I'd been avoiding my weed stores since the outbreak, figuring times were hard enough without weed paranoia, plus not wanting to dull my senses in case of another Ken String-style attack or the foreign-national engineers mobilizing against us. But it was our little ritual, so we indulged and then played around with the weapons inventory. We mimed slamming the nail sticks together in a slowly mimed sword-fight, gently and quiet. She swung one nail stick above her head, which I found hilarious, but also a little dangerous, so I told her to stop. I showed her the whiskey and how weaponization of the whiskey would work.

"One shot each?" asked Monica.

Two ounces wouldn't mean the difference between an effective whiskey torch and an ineffective one, and our weapons cache was substantial enough that the whiskey torch ranked

low in the order of weapons I'd reach for in case of attack. We each took a slug from the bottle. I grimaced, not fond of warm whiskey from a dusty bottle in the sub-basement.

Only the 27th time in terms of my personal sex act count, even in the midst of a potential world-destroying Anger outbreak, and my libido was already on the wane. I feared that after one let-down, it could be all let-downs going forward. She didn't seem to notice the downtick in hardness, so I redoubled thrusting velocity, called up a mental image of Regan, and decided to risk a trip to her compound. That got me over the edge.

12

Hypnogogicly, I had strange thoughts in a voice that was not my own.

"Dead molecules on planet Jupiter."

Hypnogogic dream-voices had spoken to me before. Everyone hears these voices. For me it had never been complete sentences, let alone sentences of intrigue. It'd been things like, "Over there," or "Not right now," little tidbits from the subconscious swimming up to the surface prior to sleep.

Then, "David Mamet collusion."

I sipped water, tried to become wakeful, hoping for a less sinister hypnogogic transition into the sleepytown. I didn't like to consider David Mamet colluding with anyone.

"Toynbee message."

"Toynbee message."

I didn't like that either. I gripped Monica. She murmured.

"In movie 2001."

"Toynbee message."

The voice was not my own head voice.

"It is not the cult of Lyndon Larouche that's responsible."

"In movie 2001."

"Resurrect dead on planet Jupiter!"

I tossed. I turned. I of course don't recall the moment sleep came, but it came. I slept. Hypnopompicly a complete message was burned into my brain:

"Toynbee message/In movie 2001/Resurrect dead/On Planet Jupiter."

That morning, Monica awoke as I placed my hand on her butt.

"Did you have bad dreams?" I asked.

"Yes."

"What were they about?"

"Toynbee converters."

"Any dead molecules?"

"On planet Jupiter," she looked at me distraught.

Was it positive or negative that we'd experienced the same delusion? Was the message of dead molecules relevant? Or was this *folie a deux*, two people with the same craziness?

We decided to have sex to take our minds off of Toynbee-related concerns, trying to keep the noise down. When the bed springs squeaked too loud we finished with the old handjob/beav-rub combo.

The household was out of bacon, but some sausage was frying. It was that internally white, unappetizing sausage that sits in freezers for months before some desperate party finally breaks down and prepares it.

I considered asking my parents about the dead molecules and David Mamet, but something kept me quiet.

Maybe I didn't want to be tied down by them. Or I didn't want Monica to be tied down either.

Monica and I played Risk. When she went to the bathroom I viewed beach bikini photos of Regan on my phone.

"Did you know David Mamet is a raging conservative now?" I asked Monica when she returned.

"I don't even know who that is."

"He wrote *Glengarry Glen Ross.*"

"What's that?"

I clicked my tongue.

"David Mamet's daughter is on the show *Girls,*" I said after a silence of some duration.

"Oh, I used to love that show when it first started," she said.

13

Our shared delusion was not the only communal strangeness. The strangest thing came from Monica's Facebook feed. The L-S-C Community Theatre Workshop's page had a YouTube video titled, *Annie Cancelled/Eyes Wide Open.*

L-S-C was hard up for entertainment. Our community theatre productions compensated for that on the largest scale possible. Our young people assumed L-S-C productions rivaled those in London and New York. I certainly used to think that anyway. There were huge ensemble casts. They even wore those little microphone wisps that the Beyonces and the Beibers of the world wore for amplification. Imagine the allure for everyone involved. Get one of those Beiber mics on your teenage daughter and she's less likely to run

screaming from L-S-C to whatever pre-Anger establishment most resembled Ray's Fuck Yard the first chance she got. The stage-struck daughters and occasional light-loafered sons of L-S-C poured their very existences into the L-S-C CTW's yearly productions. The productions lost about $10,000 a piece, even with local businesses lining up to buy overpriced ads in the wheat-paste programs. Whenever the perennial shortfall occurred and threats of "No play this year!" reared before City Council some drive or auction or otherwise community-minded extortion always raised the money.

This is what we did as a community. We staged productions of *Annie* that were good, maybe great for a small town, but poor by big town standards. Why didn't everyone just leave for the big town? That is the great mystery of L-S-C. That is why I find it unnecessary to describe Big Town happenings. Why live a small town existence, in a dream-world, only to describe Los Angeles eyeballs popped out of heads in the final act?

The YouTube video began with a brief introduction by the grand old dame of the L-S-C CTW, producer/director Leena Moran. Leena announced that she was sick of all the saccharine *Dreamcoat*s and under-realized *Tommy*s. She was an artist. Moran was an artist, Moran said straight into the digi-cam. Leena explained that she'd terminated rehearsals for *Annie* that had been ongoing for months, and had commenced rehearsals three days ago on *Leena Moran's Eyes Wide Shut*.

For the last few years the CTW had teased audiences with professional-looking trailers. The thing in L-S-C was to make the optics look like big city optics. The trailers would not improve revenue because the same people would see the plays regardless. The idea was to do the things that a *real* theatre company would do. In L-S-C that was our only goal:

to seem real; to become actualized in the face of the much realer, truly actualized external world.

This trailer failed in this regard by having the quality of a videotaped high school talent show. The frequently-concussed Lewis Orlovsky played Nick Nightingale, clunking his neurologically under-informed hands down on the piano keys. Local theatre star Steven Scapino played Bill Harford. Scapino had actually made it out of L-S-C for a while, and landed a couple commercials in New York, but Scapino needed starring roles to sustain Scapino's ego. So in one of the most self-destructive acts of folly in L-S-C history he'd scorned his working life in New York to come back to L-S-C and launch this three point boneheaded plan:

1. Write vampire novel.
2. Sell vampire novel film rights to Hollywood.
3. Direct and star in Hollywood adaptation of his vampire novel.

Friends and acquaintances viciously mocked the whole plan behind his back, although the *L-S-C Courier* reported on his plans like it was only a matter of time until he starred opposite Brad and Angelina in his vampire novel's big screen adaptation. The L-S-C Courier's policy was to believe anything typed in a press release. Scapino's Dream was the realest news they had to work with. That it could never happen was never a concern.

Anyway, there's Scapino as Bill Harford, surrounded by the masked Masonic figures from what is maybe Kubrick's most beautiful piece of set design (unless that's *Barry Lyndon*, this is open for debate) and sure the masks were crappy compared to the film's masks because of the paucity of prop

departments in L-S-C, but still, you know, they were doing their best.

As in the film, the masked Masonic figures disrobe, revealing all manner of breasts and pubic hair. Due to demos of community theatre most of the revealed breasts and pubes are of dubious legality, which in previous years had been the diametric opposite of the Leena Moran aesthetic, even though like most amateur theatre, there had always been bodices and French maid outfits and the like.

So there's Scapino/Harford surrounded by illegal breasts and beavs. The other masked members of the secret society were played by the old community theater creeps who always participated in these plays, mouthing their choral lines like those old man Muppets. I speculated the old creeps were more interested in proximity to the illegal babes than in the esteem of being one of 15.00 chorus members in *Godspell*. But having had time to reflect, maybe that is not the truth and only the projection of my warped mind.

Next, and this was just a rehearsal video mind you, the nude actresses subdue an alarmed Harford/Scapino (which is not in the original film) and Moran breaks fourth wall, runs on stage, and castrates Scapino with a box cutter. I'm thinking, "If this is rehearsal, will some prosthetic be necessary for opening night? And shouldn't the slicing of the real organ have been saved for opening or, even better, closing night?" Scapino screamed bloody murder, making it unlikely he'd be co-operative as Harford in Moran's vision from then on. Maybe realizing this and not wanting to wait is why Moran did it with full props and costumes for the trailer. She recognized her big chance to express a vision, and she expressed it.

"Poor Scapino," said Monica.

"What keeps them there?" I asked.

"I was in two of those plays. It's like a cult. Impossible to quit."

"How'd you quit then?"

"I wanted to play Volleyball instead and they were all like 'Nooooo!' and I was like, 'You guys are stupid.'"

"Are they locked in there?"

"More like it's the world they've locked out."

"Second Kubrick reference in two days," I said. "Makes you wonder if Stanley is stage-directing the whole shooting match from the great beyond."

"That would be cool," Monica said.

I unwrapped the cellophane from my Stanley Kubrick Collection box-set and popped in *Barry Lyndon* because I considered it his most challenging work, and frankly didn't believe Monica was that well-versed in Kubrick. I wanted to show her that one was not a Kubrick aficionado for having seen *A Clockwork Orange* one measly time and then having referred to it as, "So fucked up," as she had done.

14

The engineers knocked lightly on the basement window.

"What do you want?" I said peaking though the window.

"We've come to parameterize your position as a function of time," their leader said.

"No thanks," I said.

15

Monica was a trooper making it through all three hours of *Barry Lyndon*, nodding politely when I related anecdotes about the film's production history. She even seemed a little smug at the end, saying, "That could have gone on for another hour it was so good," so I popped in *2001: A Space Odyssey.* She was less of a trooper for that one. Admittedly, it was cruel to subject someone to nearly six hours of such viscerally-pounding cinema.

One unfortunate comment of hers caused me to question our whole relationship: "I thought this was supposed to be like *Star Wars.* What's up with these monkeys?"

More unfortunate was the dialogue spoken when HAL is disassembled by Dave Bowman, when HAL says, "My mind is going. I can feel it. There is no question about it. I can feel it. I can feel it." That dialogue was then stuck in my head for a 14.27-hour period. I don't mean it popped into my head from time to time. That dialogue ran as the only thought soundtrack available to me. I grunted responses to Monica and said things like, "Let's go to bed," but the thought track was composed solely of Hal's mind-loss speech, except spoken in my own mind voice. It was my mind saying, "My mind is going."

I didn't sleep, but lying in bed at least meant I didn't have to deal with Gary or anyone who'd challenge me on my mental state. When the voice ceased I took to Twitter and asked, "Anyone else get really messed up watching the end of *2001* since the outbreak?"

One reply was from TIFF's Midnight Madness programmer Colin Geddes, a response that should have made

my week, as Geddes was someone I'd read about and hoped to one day emulate, was: "Ya, don't watch that movie people. A bad idea. Not fun."

When she woke I asked Monica, "Did any of the dialogue from *2001* get stuck in your head after the movie?"

"Don't think so. Like what?"

"That part: 'My mind is going. I can feel it.'"

"That might have been the part I fell asleep for," she said.

A *tsk* sound came from me.

"I didn't like it as much. The special effects looked shitty. Like a bunch of toys against a screen."

"Monica, that is such a stupid thing to say."

She pouted. I rubbed her back, apologized and told her I loved her. Afterwards, I thought I saw Dave Bowman hiding in the closet, but it was only my old Tommy Hilfiger jacket from L-S-C's Tommy Hilfiger craze of 2003.

16

All the HJ/beav rub combos had resulted in a glut of soiled Kleenex in my bedroom waste basket. While my mom did not often come in to my room uninvited, I figured that it was possible she might and observe the offensive sperm-soaked tissue glut.

I took the sticky fibrous mass, crushed them together, wrapped one clean Kleenex around the soiled ones, peeked out my bedroom door, darted to the washroom, dropped the baseball-sized mass into the toilet and

flushed it. Sadly, the toilet filled to the brim with water. Years of experience on earth had taught me to deny my instinct to flush a second time. I searched for the plunger but it wasn't in its usual place beneath the sink. I looked in the other bathroom, perhaps the basement bathroom having needed plunging of late. Not there either. It's always embarrassing to let anyone know you need a plunger. The assumption will be that a large crap of yours has clogged the toilet.

"Dad, do you know where the plunger is?" I called out.

"Hold on," he said. He went into his bedroom, and after a moment came out with the plunger. I brushed past him and saw in his closet his own private weapons cache.

"Why was I not informed of this cache?" I asked.

"I'm not stupid. I heard you screaming about Toynbee converters in your sleep. Not the behavior of the perfectly sane," he said.

"Neither is private weapons hoarding, really," I said.

"What are you two yelling about?" my mom asked.

I pointed at the cache. After some heated debate it was agreed that my dad's bedroom cache would be split 50/50 and I'd get the 50 that didn't stay with him. He'd fashioned an impressive mace-like object out of a globe, a length of chain, and twelve razor blades. I said, "I'll start by taking the mace globe."

"That took me all night to make."

"Then the only fair thing is a draft. Since you prepared this cache you get first pick," I said.

"Fine, mace globe."

"Butcher knife," I said.

"See, given the whole Toynbee thing, that's exactly the kind of item I don't want you having in your room. One more bad dream and then in a confused waking state you'll

have us all stabbed."

"What's this about Toynbee?" asked my mom.

Monica peeked into the bedroom, I guess not wanting to breach the boundary of their matrimonial bedroom, and said, "It's this dream we both had. About dead molecules and 2001."

"Seems harmless enough," my mom said. Even this tiny disbursement of info was enough to justify her maternal protection instinct. She would rather be stabbed by an Angry me than hear aspersions cast my way.

Gary frowned. "Fine, I'll take the hockey stick with the three steak knives on the butt-end."

"Good. I'll take the softball covered in shards of broken glass," I said.

"How can you throw something like that?" asked Monica.

"There's a little patch to grip with no glass," said my dad, showing her a glass-free seam/grip area.

"Cool," she said, and inexplicably winked at Gary.

My dad straightened up, embarrassed by her weird wink, and said in a soft bass voice, "I guess that leaves me with the shoulder pads with the antique railroad spikes."

"We'd better go practice how to use these weapons," Monica said to me.

"It seems like we're preparing for war against each other. This is stupid," said mom.

Monica and I returned to my room. I stretched out on the bed and closed my eyes. Then my mom hollered, "What is all this Kleenex doing in the toilet?"

She unclogged the toilet with the plunger, which my dad then re-weaponized and kept, even though he already had a one-weapon advantage in terms of our competing caches.

17

That night, a dispute erupted over what to eat for dinner. Both Monica and I wanted beans and wieners, neither of us having had the old bean and wiener experience in some time. My mom argued that the preservatives in the wieners would make them safe to eat for weeks after another power outage, so it was best to eat the more perishable pork products first.

We settled upon Pork loin roast, even though my parents had never figured out how to cook this kind of roast, and it always got coated in gross white foam as it roasted. I made some snotty remarks about the white foam to Monica, who tried to be polite, but she couldn't help laughing when I opened the stove, scooped some foam out on a spatula and flicked it into the sink with disgust.

"That foam will make nice gravy," mom said.

"No it won't. These pork gravies always turn out all white and awful," I said.

The instinct was not to overcook the giant pork roast, but we couldn't win either way, so we overcooked it. While there was more pork than any of us were inclined to choke down, our stores of sauces (1/8th of a bottle of Diana Sauce, 1/16th of Heinz Chicken and Rib) were limited in the extreme. My dad squirted out an offensively large portion of Diana, at least 70% of the remaining 1/8th.

"Oh come on," I yelled.

"What?" asked Gary.

"That sauce has to go around!"

"Fine! Fine!" he said back, scooping some sauce up on a spoon and flinging it down on my alabaster pork.

"How do you know I even wanted that sauce? Maybe I wanted the Chicken and Rib."

"I see Mrs. Robertson has burned a large pentagram into her front lawn," my mom said to change the subject.

"We've all seen that," I said.

Gary had calmed down after the Diana Sauce row. "Son, I've been thinking. Weapons caches are all well and good, but we need to escalate our fitness regimen. How about a friendly family competition downstairs after dinner?"

"You want to do it because you'll win," I said in a loud voice, "Because you do a bunch of push-ups every day, and I don't believe in exercise."

"Sounds like a fun idea," my mom said.

"Sounds all too mandatory," I said.

"For sure," said Monica, always big on the gym, pre-A.D., hence the hotness of her bod.

"Everyone is against me," I said, "Nothing new."

The three of them did burpees, Gary shouting encouragement and for all I know slapping Monica's butt in encouragement while I sat in front of the TV watching my DVD of Kubrick's second feature *The Killing* and surreptitiously eating a raw hot dog.

18

I wrote a short screenplay:

Exterior. Golf Course. 18th Green. The Iowa Gambler is lining up a 20-foot putt. Neck-Beard Muldoon is lining up an 18-foot putt.

The Iowa Gambler: "They don't call me the Iowa Gambler because I'm from Iowa, or because I'm a gambler, they call me that because I sink long putts."

Neck-Beard Muldoon: "They don't call me Neck-Beard Muldoon because of my grotesque neck-beard, they call me that because I *always* make long putts."

I showed it to Monica.
     "Not bad," she said.
     I showed it to my mom.
     "Pretty funny," she said, but did not laugh.
     "I don't get it," Gary said.
     "Figures," I said.

19

Pierre had been a comfort to us. Lying underfoot as Monica and I watched a movie; positioned serenely on his bed, feigning disinterest but hoping a morsel might fall at dinner; sniffing; eventually learning newspaper peeing was acceptable.

He made Monica feel at home. Dogs do not express awkward emotions. Their aggression is active, not passive. A dog who likes you will lick your palm, rest the full weight of his head on your knee, or show his belly. The dog resting comfortably against Monica's thighs made her seem like a

part of the household instead of a young concubine dumped into our dwelling merely as a result of my end times lust.

Nor was Pierre a burden in terms of food consumption, for we did not consider the dark day of appropriating Pierre's kibble for human consumption. His extra-large bag of Fromm's Adult Gold promised to last him for months.

As we watched my least favourite Kubrick film, *Full Metal Jacket,* Monica absent-mindedly stroking behind his ears, Pierre reared and showed his teeth, which I'd only seen him do a couple times in territorial food positionings vs. visiting dogs.

"Pierre!" I shouted and poked Pierre's hind-quarter like the Dog Whisperer. He turned on me, jaw and haunches vibrating with fear and hate. My dad made the scene and took the Dog Whisperer technique to the next level, grabbing Pierre by the middle, and holding him down on his back, which Pierre did not enjoy. Pierre squirmed away and tore a chunk out of my dad's wrist. Shocking us all, my dad punched Pierre straight in the skull, dazing Pierre. We then locked Pierre in his cage.

Dream-dog noises, little squeaks like he was chasing a rabbit, reminded us of his depth of consciousness and cast a pall over dinner. He alternated between a mournful whine and a ferocious snarl. We had not considered Angry animals, but Googling "Angry animals" provided examples and bloody images. The unspoken consensus = 'Give Pierre the benefit of the doubt for the time being.'

Post-carnality that night, Monica and I were lying on our blanket and listening to the tail end of *Bruce Springsteen Live 1975 – 1985* when Pierre burst through the sub-basement/basement door—an impossibility, since dogs lack the ability to twist handles or clasp compressible knobs. He lunged for Monica's neck. I caught him mid-air in a weird

kind of man-on-dog full-nelson as he ripped into her calf. A moment later my dad ran down swinging his mace-globe and expertly bonked Pierre, managing not to bonk the very nearby me.

And so RIP Pierre. 14.36 years old. A silent, loving companion through the tumult of my adolescence. A happy, tail-wagging guy. A being I considered possessed of wisdom and grace who set an example for us all, somehow, despite being a dog. A beagle with whom I had shared most of my existence, dumped in the secret of night to rot beside Ken String's corpse.

My mother and I embraced and wept openly, all while Monica stood bleeding from her neck and calf wearing nothing but bra and panties due to our recent sex-focus.

"You can put your clothes on already," I said, unfair since she'd been badly wounded and traumatized. My mom applied alcohol to Monica's wounds out of necessity, not passive aggression, and dressed Monica's neck wound using our very limited supply of tensor bandages. Monica's calf wound was dressed using six regular sized Band-Aids, of which we had dozens.

RIP to my man Pierre.

20

After everyone had gone to sleep I visited the sub-basement, drank dusty whiskey, smoked many bowls of weed and looked at old Facebook photos of Pierre on my phone. Probably the dumbest thing I could have done.

I passed out on the cold cement floor and woke at 2:02:45 am to a horrible recollection of just who I was. Lloyd MacDonald, with all the gross associated remembrances of what it meant to be Lloyd MacDonald: cruelties inflicted by and upon me; absurdities; gross outs; the odd bout of suicidal ideation; lash-outs and let downs; squandered friendships and burned down opportunities; my smattering of small triumphs—to have lived a life as a person who'd made a poor impression on the world.

With my hangover I welcomed the proposition of not being Lloyd MacDonald for too many more mornings of waking up to several spam emails, but no emails from anyone who actually cared. Fuck this, I, Lloyd, thought, and stumbled to my bed. Monica must have felt my regret of being alive, regret of being Lloyd, and she joined forces with me to suggest that it was indeed worth being alive/Lloyd. When the creaking got too loud we went to the floor. After which, the sadness came right back, the knowledge of what I had always been. Sex is a sanctuary to which a kid can never trust himself for long.

21

After toast and pancakes, a breakfast that suffered from a redundancy of starches and a total absence of proteins, I brought my laptop to my room by myself, which always looked suspicious. I could have been using the laptop for

anything: writing screenplays, creating hilarious memes, Liking a status, but the laptop seemed stamped with the red letter of self-gratification whenever I carried it to my private chamber.

Hangovers had always produced in me a day-long randiness and a corresponding uptick in the depravity of my desires. On these days I sought out the more esoteric pornographic categories, taking comfort in the lower depths of human sexual inclination.

A Facebook post from Regan deepened my thirst for wickedness.

> "Dudes! Impotent as a result of Anger? It happens. It's happening here chez Regan daily. Not to worry. The foolproof solution is called I'll stick my fingers up your butts. You might think you are too manly for that BUTT it works."

How crass and horrid, I thought, of both the pun and the whole proposition.

I sought out butt fingering pornography and wondered if I desired to have my own butt fingered. My anus had not yet been breached by me for reasons concerned largely with hygiene, so I viewed butt fingering videos with curiosity, occasionally minimizing them to view a photo of Regan in a bikini, and then sort of magically overlaying her image over the moving image of the onscreen female butt fingerer.

After more or less exhausting this category on Pornhub, I had a coughing fit, my whole body trying to expel the degenerate instincts cancering my soul. A rush of wholesome memories of Regan seized me. How

sweet and kind she looked. Her flare for silliness. Her self-confidence borne of richness and good looks. How she'd not always been some A.D.'d maniac advertising butt fingerings.

Taking advantage of her in her corrupt state would be a low-point. Would I be called to account in front of Pearly Gates for either fantasizing of a Reganian butt fingering, or for actually risking life and limb to receive one from an Angry Regan Jefferson?

I looked at her big smiling teeth in the yearbook. Was that person gone? Did I want to use the husk of her physical form to avenge outdated, unfulfilled fantasies? Did an Anger disease make that acceptable? Was this my own specific manifestation of the A.D., and had it been festering in me since some early time, since rejection planted the seed?

My blood circulated by way of seventy-five pushups. I actually did exercise quite frequently, but only in private. Having vocalized years of stringent anti-exercise views v. Gary it would have appeared hypocritical of me were I found out.

Later I washed my butt better than usual in the shower, hoping Monica could meet my new unpleasant need and spare me a trip to Regan's compound, the risk that entailed, and the shame involved in using Regan's Angry husk.

"Put your finger in my butt," I instructed Monica, later, coitally.

"I'd rather not," she said.

I then stuck my own finger in my butt, but felt stupid reaching back like that, and after we had a big fight. In the next room my parents' own bed springs creaked, which I could not recall ever having heard before.

22

I headed downstairs to get away from Gary's audible thrusts.

When down in the dumps I often took refuge in the social media content of inferior peers—people living in trailers outside L-S-C's town limits; those for whom a used truck served as a profile picture; people who paid for things with a lot of dimes and nickels and said "I'll just have to pay with change." But those types weren't uploading actively anymore so I did my first big sweep of the international news landscape.

Many stories seemed fraudulent, the products of Angry minds. But spread among the false headlines, some bloggers were still reporting what they were witnessing, and a few major outlets' intrepid journalists were stowed away, committed to posting factual updates despite peril.

I took them all in as one big carcinogenic breath, highlights included:

- The return of the Mothman. Many Mothman sightings.
- Harlot the Witch. For one night only at Ray's Fuck Yard.
- A Fire Tornado in Tennessee that killed 10,000 in a big spiraling flame.
- Charismatic leader emerges in Eastern Europe/Former Military Strong Man Way More Charismatic Of Late.
- Crumbling physical infrastructure.
- Mass Exoduses. Exodai?
- Ugly ugly scenes on on- and off-ramps.
- CN Tower cracked in two, with the top tip falling to the ground and lying phallic along Front Street.
- All NBA Games Cancelled!

- David Lynch suggests collective Transcendental Meditation experiment to halt Anger.
- Run on pharmacies, but not banks.
- Hoax cures for the Anger disease like 'Drink two Red Bulls, half a can of tomato juice, smoke three cigarettes.'
- Worse behavior from men than women, experts observe.
- Films causing unprecedented number of psychic breaks, best not to watch any.
- Ray's Fuck Yard trending worldwide for three days straight and lots of funny RFY 4chan content as a result, because of such a well-loved logo of Farmer Ray being appropriated in filthy ways.
- Horrible GIFs: GIFs of beheadings; coprophagiac GIFs like you'd have hoped not to see.
- Snipers on condo balconies the norm, not the exception.
- Dog Whisperer Caesar Milan Murders 120 dogs.
- Cult of Bob Dylan emerges after death of Bob Dylan.
- Pale Riders beheld.
- Bird invasions.
- Swimming pools red with blood, whether real blood or mystery blood no one knows.
- Whales all beach themselves on various coasts.
- Shadow people exit shadows, become real people, seem disoriented and ill-tempered.
- Dog-men, as in man's body/dog's head, in trenchcoats like old-time wise-guys, smoking cigarettes. Imagine— visit your local gas station to pillage sundries and a dog-man stands there like he owns the place.
- Strange booms heard the world over. Rumours that the Anger started in the prisons because all at once the prisons had it at a 99% capacity, guards and inmates alike.

- Perdition widespread.
- Harlot women in wilderness as well as cities—as in, go into the bush, find a harlot woman.
- Many claimants claiming 100% proof of their claims.
- Hairless dogs growing hair.
- Nuclear explosions in middle-east an hourly phenomenon.
- Bluish mist consumes Rochester, perhaps related to Chicago mist.
- Marauders marauding somewhat safer suburbs.
- Olympic athlete laments wasting life training for stupid Olympics.
- People shooting off fireworks not helping anyone's nerves at the moment, thanks.
- Ten Things Only Angry People Will Understand trends.
- 250 earthquakes.
- Multiple fireballs visible from Jupiter, has astronomy world buzzing. (Dead molecules?)
- WWE continues broadcasts, introduces faux-Angry stable of heels, until a heel called Big E. Langston legitimately becomes Angry and kills six with a razor taped to his wrist on the main event of *Monday Night Raw*.
- No news on medical condition of Steven Scapino, here, locally.
- Particle accelerator at CERN to blame for this? Either way, CERN burned to ground by angry mob.
- Mystery ash spewed into atmosphere.
- Lineups of big-wigs outside Underground Bases waiting to be let in.
- Blood runs on streets of Saskatoon a horse's bridle high.

- Discourse grows increasingly scatological, such that pictures of people's own poop are being uploaded all over Instagram.
- Adamnan was right, some think.
- Anger rationalizers ask questions on Reddit like, "Is it Acceptable to be Angry?"
- Ugbogiorinmwin breathes fire outside Toronto Reference Library.
- Prophetic personas like John Hoagland say they saw this coming all along.
- Chimaera takes Times Square.
- Blood pours forth from nearly every elevator.
- Telex from someone inside an Underground Base reads: "No need to lineup outside, the Anger is in here too."
- Demon intelligence reported in super computers.
- Having failed to predict the Anger, Sylvia Browne admits to being a phony.
- Mysterious number of unmanned boring machines bore away at downtown Detroit intersection.
- One in three people in Lowell, Massachusetts suddenly suffer from Morgellons.
- Chthonic sightings on the rise.
- L. Ron Hubbard reincarnated as guy who looks exactly like the young LRH.
- Netflix numbers spike despite warnings that movies are causing bad psychic mojo.
- esdc.gc.ca I.T. Guy hangs himself with Ethernet cable.
- Marks of Al Jassaca and Ankou spotted.
- LinkedIn reports not one visit, not one person, even by accident, for four days.

23

I woke weakened by systemic lethargy. I noticed Monica's mole. A mole that I had found charming in our early days together, but was increasingly repulsed by. The mole would sprout hairs as she grew older. A neighbor of mine had once tried to clip a mole of hers off with nail clippers, but it bled badly and she'd been hospitalized, and somehow I associated this horror with Monica's mole.

As Monica began snoring, I woke her up with a shake. "What?" she asked.

"You were snoring."

"So."

"So it's gross."

She closed her eyes and resumed snoring. I woke her again. "Can you at least roll over and turn your head the other way?"

When she did, I considered the thousand lonely nights I'd spent, crotch against pillow, hoping for such a companion, yet already I was taking her for granted, horrified by moles and nasal blockages. Had Monica not been stuck with me I could have pined and felt tragic, instead I breathed in bad breath, dog dead, parents loudly fornicating just metres away.

Her lack of introspection regarding the A.D. was galling to me. Whenever I broached the topic she affected a breezy air, like it was a snowstorm cancelling school for the day, but the snow was melting and normal bus routes would resume shortly. She must have known these were end times, yet no noted uptick in her personal profundity followed. Perhaps being 16.25 prevents profundity during even the darkest hours. Maybe I'd have been better off with an older woman. Maybe Mrs. Robertson was on the market haha.

I did pushups on the floor hoping Monica wouldn't wake and witness my hypocrisy. The pushups did not alleviate my dysthymia. I opened a biography of Ed Gein, but that was ghoulish reading material during the effective Geinification of mankind. What pulsed and throbbed in your Gein-like monsters had been buried within us all along, but now it was spreading like a pool of milk.

"Screw this," I thought, and decided to traverse the riotous streets in pursuit of Regan's bod, still advertised as being available.

24

Throughout that afternoon my feelings towards Monica oscillated between mild affection and coal-grey hatred. She made a throat-clearing noise until I said, "Can you please stop clearing your throat?"

"Sorry, I didn't realize I'm not allowed to clear my throat."

Lack of purpose fuelled my hostility. Inane as call centre work and community college studies were, they kept the mind occupied. I decided to work on a new screenplay.

Exterior - Regan's Compound

Lloyd arrives and sees a lengthy cue for Regan's bod-usage. Regan's brother Rex approaches and hands Lloyd a ticket.

Lloyd: How long of a wait?

Rex: About 35 minutes.

Montage of Lloyd whistling, Lloyd kicking a pine cone, Lloyd flipping a coin to illustrate passage of time.

Lloyd: I've been waiting a long time for this.

Guy in Line: Tell me about it. Regan is the hottest. Even Angry, this is going to be the best five minutes of my life.

An Angry arrives and tries to bypass the line; he is shot and killed by Rex.

Rex: Darn, third one today.

Montage of Lloyd doing little shoulder and arm isometrics, tenting his fingers, stretching to again illustrate passage of time.

Rex: Alright Lloyd you're up.

Interior – Regan's Fuck Room. Regan is seated on a small couch, waiting.

Lloyd: Regan.

Regan: Lloyd.

Lloyd: Describe your level of cleanliness.

Regan: After each patron I use a Playtex Fresh and Sexy Wipe.

Lloyd: Shall we get down to business?

Lloyd gets down to business, mounting, some thrusts, some embarrassed noises.

Regan: Having trouble?

Lloyd: Well...

Regan: Perhaps a butt fingering?

Lloyd: Have never been much of a butt-fingering man but...under the circumstances...

A loud throat clear broke my concentration.

"Can't you see I'm working here?"

"On what?"

"A screenplay."

"Like it will ever get made."

"That is not the point of art. The point of art is the thrill of creation, something you wouldn't understand, sitting there, doing that Search-A-Word on famous bodies of water."

She brightened, "I have an idea. Let's make it on your video camera! What's it about?"

"Never mind that."

I reread the document, emailed it to my Gmail account, and deleted it from my hard-drive.

Supper was beans only, no protein except for bean protein, hardly enough protein for my tastes or Gary's.

"Could've used more meat," Gary said, "How about we raid the Strings?"

"Gary!" said my mom.

"What? We know Ken is out of the picture," said Gary.

"We rob from his poor children?" asked my mom.

"Just check out the situation," said Gary.

"Absolutely not," she said.

I disengaged for the rest of the night, barely focusing on *Lolita*, except to express dismay when Monica said, "I don't really like these classical ones as much," because by *classical* she meant *black and white*.

Regan's Facebook update read: "To expedite matters we've taken a lesson from the porn industry, gangbang porn specifically, and we now use Emerald as Regan's fluffer. If you don't know what this means it means that Emerald jerks you off while you're in line for Regan."

Emerald was attractive as her older sister, and also not a one-time friend of mine. She even resembled Sue Lyon to some minor degree. It seemed gross that Regan now referred to herself in the third person, and this pushed me over the edge. This was not the Regan I had known. It was no time for moralistic hand-wringing. Nothing more than enjoying the hot zombified bod of a girl I had always needed and not got. To cement my decision, and I guess out of some misdirected spite towards Monica, I commented on Regan's latest post, "On my way!"

After Monica fell asleep I snuck from my bed, and rolled the car slowly and silently out of the driveway in neutral.

Mrs. Robertson again waved. She wore no shirt. It was a 25-minute drive under ideal circumstances, so I budgeted an hour. Angries had set up a barricade on Carlton Street, but it was a low-quality barricade that I easily drove around on the paved shoulder. The Angries held up clubs and baseball bats and hooted in anger at being outsmarted so easily.

A flaming, overturned cop car had to be steered around. Some youthful wretches fired upon the CRV with a B.B. gun, but the B.B.s only hit the bumper and caused no structural damage. The streets were calmer than expected. No Chimaeras wreaking havoc. No Ugbogiorinmwins breathing fire. Some ash in the atmosphere, but nothing too toxic to breathe. I passed a travelling circus. And then another travelling circus. And then another travelling circus. And then another travelling circus. And then another travelling circus. And then another travelling circus. And then another

travelling circus. And then another travelling circus, which must have been some kind of delusion or else break in the space-time continuum, because why so many travelling circuses all of a sudden?

I considered swerving around the man swinging nun-chuks in the middle of one intersection, but then feared he'd strike my window with his chucks, so I side-swiped him into a drainage ditch. RIP nun-chuks man, presumably, as he looked kind of frail to begin with.

Turning down the road leading to Regan's compound I received a Facebook message from her.

OMG Lloyd. I have locked myself in my parents pantry for the past three days. My brothers have gone crazy. They are using those gross FB messages to lure people to the compound, then killing everyone. They are going to kill you if you come. They are up in our old tree fort picking each new person off with a rifle. You have to save me Lloyd. Do you have a gun? If so you need to come in the back way, park down the street, cut through my neighbours back-

yard and you'll have to shoot them before they know what's going on. They aren't my brothers anymore. If it works yell out, "It's me Lloyd, I got them." and I'll come out. And Lloyd. I'm hoping you aren't Angry. And I don't blame you for saying you are coming to take advantage of the situation because I'm willing to give you the benefit of the doubt and assume you were also giving me the benefit of the doubt and planned to rescue me all along.

I debated heading home. But here was the prototypical adolescent fantasy—fighting off cadres of assailants so that a beautiful girl might love you. To save Regan. The plan was to wound Regan's brothers with my 22, and then send them out of the game with the shotgun. Were I sent out of the game it would be Regan's dignity I left the game for, as good a way to go as any in these turbulent times.

25

Driving down the private road was a different matter. Gravel sprayed upward, and only having been to Regan's house once, I wasn't sure which neighbour's driveway she meant. She did not respond to my nervously typed text of, "Was totally coming to rescue you@@@@!!!! Which neighbour's driveway@@@"

Twice I debated a three-point turn in one of the driveways leading to Regan's. What kept me going was the ghost of high school, a period I was not even two years removed from, yet a period I knew I would never escape.

I'd had good friends. That had been most destructive to me. The sardonic clown role only precluded me from the A1,

Regan-type babes; it did not preclude me from the camarade-
rie I experienced with my crowd. The disconnect began on a
short trip after high school. In a Cambridge, Mass coffee house
I dug the bereted and lamented L-S-C's lack of legitimate coffee
houses. I considered myself a Cambridge, Mass man trapped in
a culture-free zone. Upon my return I could only scoff at existences built around sports and television. I lashed out. I stopped
calling people, and soon they stopped calling me. A year later
I was fully ostracized, and could only scrape up companionship
from the absolute lowest Calcofluco classes.

I began to dream of Dan Good, whom I had known all
my life; A.G. Rigopolous, with whom I'd laughed till tears
in tents we had constructed; the other guys. I had tried to
call them, tried to explain that my verbal lashings had been
a big misunderstanding, that we should all get together, re-
form the curling team, go for wings, etc. But it was too late.
L-S-C was desperate for villains.

Regan was not Dan Good. Regan was not A.G. Rigopolous. But through the same magic I applied to her
Facebook photos I hoped she might become a portal back
in time, the same way Ralph Lauren Original Polo Cologne
takes me back in a painful way.

26

I crept out of the car and traversed the remaining 100 yards
on foot. It was a moonless night. From two homes before
Regan's the glow of smartphones could be seen in a tree fort.

Shotguns only being effective at close range, I crept and crept, taking less than two steps a minute, not wanting some twig to snap untowardly and foil the whole mission. I aimed the rifle at a smartphone's glow and fired. Robbie fell from the treehouse, and landed on his neck, out of the game.

I felt a moment's remorse for Robbie, recalling one time he had picked me third in a game of rugby, even though several other dudes were more skilled, so maybe he'd been trying to send some message of tolerance and inclusion.

I fired again and Rex yelled, "I'm blind. I'm blind."

I removed the shotgun from the strap that held it to my back and commenced the most dangerous part of the mission, climbing the tree-nailed steps to finish off Rex, who could have been lying in wait. Fortunately, Rex was only convulsing, so I sprayed shot right at his temple. Due to aspects of physics that I am ill-equipped to describe, a piece of Rex's grey matter shot up and grazed my lip. No amount of sleeve-wiping could null that sensation, so I had to put it out of my mind.

I entered the home and yelled, "Regan, it's me, Lloyd!"

"Lloyd, is that you?" she asked from the kitchen pantry.

"Yes, it's me, Lloyd," I yelled.

"Oh thank God! Are they dead?"

Emerald sobbed from behind the couch. Regan ran out and hugged me. It felt as good as all those high school hugs I'd catalogued and called upon. She embraced Emerald and said, "They are back to normal now. In heaven. That wasn't really them these last few days. They are out of their misery now."

"Cooler!" I barked at Regan, feeling like an effective man. She didn't move.

"Cooler! We need to pack your proteins."

"Right, um, whatever, sure."

"No, for real. My base is seriously short on proteins. We need all of yours to survive."

They filled a cooler with the high-end proteins the Jeffersons were accustomed to. Venison sausage, Cornish hens, turkeys for their sheer meat volume. I commanded a traumatized Emerald to pack canned goods in suitcases.

A car pulled into the driveway.

"I'll handle this," I said, and reloaded the shotgun.

Outside was my high school acquaintance J.P. Scalipi.

"Lloyd, what are you doing here?" he asked.

"Rescuing these poor girls. What are you doing here?"

"Same."

"Ya right. Get the hell out of here," I said, and pointed the weapon at him.

"So the body-use thing…"

"You aren't using anyone's body today J.P.," I said with the moral fervor of a man who had not thirty minutes ago been interested in a bod-use himself.

"Fine, fine," he said, "It's only that I drove all the way here and…"

"You've got to be kidding," I said, aiming the gun.

J.P. Scalipi decamped peacefully.

A white Suburban tore up the road and fishtailed into the driveway. Another guy we'd known from high school, Anthony Mancuso, jumped out, waving two paring knives in the air, yelling, "Faaaaacebooooook." I sent him straight out of the game.

We drove with purpose, like in a video game. Regan sat in the passenger seat, Emerald in back, weeping. The many travelling circuses were nowhere to be seen, which didn't bode well with respect to my mental health.

Near my house Regan said to Emerald, "Emerald, put your earphones in and shut your eyes."

I pulled to the side of the road. Regan kissed my mouth. I reached eagerly for one boob and she pulled away. She said, "Come on Lloyd," grossed out by and disappointed in how I'd spoiled my hero-reward moment. Even in end times, post-daring rescue, I am blowing it, I thought.

The household was not asleep. All household lights were on. We carried in the coolers and suitcases of provisions.

"Provisions," I announced, trying to frame the narrative.

"Lloyd, we can't be operating rescue missions for every female acquaintance you've ever known," Gary said.

Regan waved to my mom, "Hi, we met once."

Mom disregarded this.

"Let's unpack these proteins," I said to Gary, trying to steer the narrative back in the direction of proteins.

"I'm glad you're home safe," my mom finally said.

"Where will they sleep?" Gary asked.

"We can sleep on the floor," Regan offered.

"Floor in my room," I said, and then, regrettably, "Like a sleepover."

My mom appeared physically ill, and then said, "Llyod, this is not a flophouse."

"Flophouse?" Monica asked, not knowing what a flophouse was, but not liking the connotation.

I tossed a pack of venison sausage to Gary, "Should be good for breakfast huh Dad?"

He muttered and unpacked provisions.

The four of us went to my room. Emerald, though .498630138697 of a year younger than Monica, was more popular, rich, and acne-free, so she existed in a different universe altogether. Still, they embraced like long-lost friends.

Both Jefferson girls wanted showers and towels. During their showers I brought up the comforter that Monica and I

usually laid over the basement floor for our sexual exchanges and laid it on my hardwood bedroom floor.

"Tomorrow night I can blow up the air mattress," I said to Monica, but Monica wasn't speaking to me.

After their showers we turned out the lights and went to sleep. In the middle of the night a whiny Emerald asked Monica if she could sleep beside her on the bed. Monica acquiesced. So it went, from East to West—Emerald, Monica, me, with Monica separating me from Emerald, keeping things relatively civilized. I fell back asleep and when I woke up Regan was curled in front of me. So then it went Emerald, Monica, Me, Regan. And I woke in the physiological condition I almost always woke in, which was with a serious boner, and the boner was pressed into a sleeping Regan, and I thought, "This is quite the situation here."

27

I'd had a painful boil on my forehead all this time. After waking up in a Monica/Regan sandwich I felt a small river of pus and blood pouring from it. I excused myself and spent a solid twenty-five minutes squeezing and sopping up black blood and bile in the bathroom. It looked red and irritated after, so my mom's concealer was put to work.

When I returned the three girls were cuddled together on the bed. It was heartening to witness how girls can form sisterhoods in seconds when necessary. On the floor I started doing pushups.

"I thought you didn't exercise," Monica said.

"I do sometimes. In secret," I said, "But with the rise in the population of this room it's hard to keep secrets any longer."

"Why in secret?" Regan asked.

"Oh, Gary and I had this dispute years ago where I took a really firm anti-exercise stance."

"Chow time!" Gary yelled from the kitchen.

Regan and Emerald exited my room wearing tank tops. If the tank tops did not have the stomach-covering part, they would have been bras. They were those kinds of tank top. I thought this might inflame tensions, but I didn't want to say anything and seem like a perv. Upon seeing them, Gary choked on his corn-beef hash.

"Wow, corn beef hash and venison sausage," I said, once more trying to steer conversation in the direction of our recent protein boon.

"I couldn't resist," said Gary.

"I wanted to save that corn beef because it came in a can," said my mom.

Everyone took a sausage, some hash.

"Never had this kind of sausage for breakfast before," Emerald said in a half-observation/half-complaint.

The sausage squirted grease as I cut into it. I wiped the grease off my cheek with a napkin, and used this as an excuse to dab at my leaking boil, where I could feel an accumulation of moisture.

My mom gave me this hand signal we had that meant, "Let's have the story" or otherwise, "Get on with the story already."

"Very little story," I said, "Saw on Facebook that Regan was in trouble, and decided I could not sit idly by."

"Is that why you posted a comment on her Facebook page that made no reference to saving her?" asked Monica.

"Damn hackers," I said, "Taking advantage of end times confusion to impugn the truly innocent."

"Lloyd, you can't be taking the car to save all your friends. What if you'd been captured? We'd be without a car," said Gary.

"Fine, no more rescues," I said.

"I've hidden the keys," said Gary, "This is a trust issue Lloyd."

Brooding above hash, I dabbed at my forehead again with my napkin and frowned at the orangey grease and blood still secreting from me.

Regan spoke up. "My brothers went crazy. Lloyd had to shoot them."

At this Emerald broke down again and everyone's hash consumption went on hiatus as Regan and Monica attended to her with sisterly female attentions. Despite her flophouse concern my mom also got in on the bonding by dampening a cloth and handing it to Emerald who was I suppose supposed to cool her forehead with it, though she just held it in her hand.

"It was for the best," Regan said, "They weren't themselves anymore."

The boil's output was on the decline, only outputting clear oil mixed with a little makeup. I hoped to be done oozing by the end of breakfast. I cursed the fluorescent light above me.

Emerald asked my mom if she'd seen any rageheads.

"Yes, our neighbour Ken String. And if you look out the window you see our other neighbour Mrs. Robertson doing bad things to herself with a stick. Ugh, what am I saying? You don't want to see that."

But they did. All except Gary looked out the still-unboarded window at Mrs. Robertson doing the bad things. I

thought I caught Gary glance in the direction of the Regan/ Emerald combo's collective thigh/buttocks area.

"Lloyd. I am proud of you for keeping a cool head and bringing back these provisions," said Gary, "But one thing I am less proud of is that you didn't bring back any ice trays. You know we only have three ice trays and desperately need more."

"Geez, sorry Gary," I said.

"It's not your fault Lloyd. I'm sure you were under a lot of pressure," said my mom, "But there is one thing. I don't want all four of you in that bedroom. It's weird. I'll make you girls a bed in the basement."

"Mom!" I cried, and immediately cringed at the childish petulance in my voice. I hoped she only meant the Jeffersons, and that I'd still be allowed to share a bed with my official romantic partner Monica.

"Oh relax Lloyd," my mom said, and the women chuckled in a solidification of their new woman-bond.

After a bit, Gary said, "You know, Lloyd has brought more girls home since this Anger disease than he did in the entire period of his life prior to the Anger disease."

I left the table in a huff to affect final ministrations to my boil ooze.

28

Boil ooze ministrations complete, I joined the three girls downstairs and suggested a viewing of *A Clockwork Orange*. This was not greeted with enthusiasm. Monica's tastes were

now the majority tastes. We watched *Hot Teen Vampires* on Emerald's phone instead. I thought of the David Lynch quote about "watching a movie on a fucking telephone" and how it is "such a sadness," but did not share this because the numbers skewed against me, and I didn't want to seem negative in already tough times.

I watched a few minutes of *A Clockwork Orange* with the headphones in, but with no one to point out production history anecdotes to it got stale fast. I squeezed onto the couch to take in some *HTV*, but mostly to squeeze onto the couch. Regan leaned her head against my arm in a nonchalant way that Monica pretended not to notice. Regan asked to see the sub-basement weapons cache.

After showing her the whiskey and how to weaponize it, we sat in the fort that Dan Good and I had built beneath the stairs as pre-pubescents.

"How is Dan?" she asked.

"I'm not sure. I haven't talked to him in a while."

"You should call him."

I wouldn't reveal that I could not call Dan. The last time I'd tried he'd hung up on me, and the time before that he'd hung up on me. All because of the incident at the East Ender. But I couldn't resist regaling her with stories of our shared youth, of our various operations and fantasies, plots and cruelties. Dan had been on her level, popularity-wise, and I always found myself reverting to this pathetic state around superior peers, beginning every sentence, "My friend Dan and I..." something I'd been doing since grade nine to ensure that no one could forget we were friends. He'd downplayed our friendship publicly because I presented no strategic advantage to him as he'd climbed the ranks, even while every night we talked on the phone for hours, which was weird, I suppose, for heterosexual male adolescents to do.

"How will you know if he's alive if you don't call him?" she asked.

"He's probably dead. Archambeault is dead. Rigopolous dead. Ken String dead. My dog dead. Us soon too."

An unwanted wave of emotion came over me. For the first time the Anger felt real. It was not a whacky thing related to Dennis Hopper or travelling circuses. It was the unspooling of all we'd experienced. Though raised Catholic, my faith was insubstantial. But a fear of hell had stuck with me from early teachings. I felt like the thousand years of tribulation was upon us. I would never reconcile with Dan Good, and what if the tribulation was not 11-foot beasts kicking your head off in Hades and then the head re-growing and the beasts kicking it off again and the beasts hating you because you were one of God's creatures and they hated God, but rather the thousand years of tribulation would be bad dreams of me calling Dan Good and Dan Good hanging up, of the look Archambeault gave me when I tried to buy him a beer in a bar one time, two-months post-lashings, a look of, "Don't even think about it." This was the hell I feared most, so it wasn't doing me any good to be sitting in the sub-stair fort Dan and I spent crucial developmental years trading baseball cards in.

Regan put her arm around me. A breast of hers pressed into my shoulder, which, despite all this eschatological doom, was a pleasant sensation for the old shoulder.

"Lloyd," she said, "You came there to save me. Even if you didn't know it at the time. It was God's plan for us."

"Sorry about your brothers."

"Me too."

We drank dusty whiskey. "To Rex and Robbie," I said.

"To Dan Good," she said.

29

As the girls' dug into *Hot Teen Vampires 2* I snooped through Regan and Emerald's suitcases in my room. Noticing a number of high-end bras in Regan's bag, I wondered if Regan's impressive bust was not an illusion created by expensive brassieres. I took off my shirt and put one on. For good measure I put on a pair of Emerald's underpants. I began to relieve the tension that had accumulated in me. There was a knock at the door.

"Hold on!" I said.

"Let me in," said Monica.

"One second."

"What are you doing in there?"

"Nothing, hold on a second," I said, scrambling to put undergarments back in the bags as I'd found them.

"Man you are gross," she said.

30

Monica retrieved the hair scrunchy she was looking for without speaking to me. I dropped in on my parents. My mom was reading and my dad was timing how quickly he could complete a Rubik's cube.

"What's your best time so far?" I asked, hoping to renew goodwill between us.

"Seven minutes."

Not a particularly great time, but I let it slide.

Downstairs, I said to Regan, "Maybe you should post a picture on Facebook, both to let your Friends know you're alright and to let them know the bod-use statuses of previous days were a hoax."

"Already clarified the hoax," she said.

"Maybe a pic to let everyone know you're safe and sound at the MacDonald household."

"If we're taking pictures I have to get changed," Emerald said.

The girls dressed for pictures in my room while I reapplied concealer to my boil. Girls of their respective ages were well-versed in the art of the selfie, so I was confident the pics wouldn't be taken with an unflattering flash. Regan and Emerald looked classy as all-get-out. Regan in an off-white Cashmere sweater and Emerald in a t-shirt with a picture of William S. Burroughs and David Bowie on it.

"Emerald! Did not know you were a Burroughs fan!" I said.

"Who?" she asked.

"The guy on your shirt."

"I don't know who those guys are. I just like shirts with faces on them."

"I see. Well, if you do become interested I have a copy of *Cities of the Red Night* upstairs which I might lend you."

"I think I'm good," said Emerald.

The four of us squeezed into one picture, with Monica and me in behind and the sisters up front. Within seconds it was posted to Regan's wall, and shared by Monica and Emerald. The Likes amassed quickly.

Emerald selected an episode of some wealth-worshipping commercial pabulum they'd moved on to.

"Hey Lloyd," Regan said, "Maybe one of just the two of us for old times' sake."

I beamed. Monica didn't quite glower but revealed a self-contained anger that would maybe constitute 1/10th of a glower. We took the pic and both uploaded it to FB, where I made it my profile picture.

The sun shone in through the basement windows. The temperature was 12 degrees Celsius, a very warm day for early April in L-S-C, the kind that always prompted barbecues and other "you-can-never-hold-back-Spring"-type celebrations. It was Good Friday, which we'd all forgotten, because the only thing that signified Good Friday for us had been the civic holiday. Regan asked if we could go outside.

"Better not. Mrs. Robertson, the Strings…" I said.

But we did anyway. Without saying anything to my parents the four of us crept out and stood on the deck, took deep breaths, and smelled new earth.

"Quick game of Frisbee?" I asked.

I have always loved the flight of the Frisbee. What maybe made me miss my old gang the most was a dearth of suitable Frisbee opponents.

"What should we do if an Angry person comes?" Emerald asked.

"Try to look Angry yourself," I said.

The girls all practiced looking Angry. Monica's Angry impression was the funniest.

Gary came out and admonished, "What do you think you're doing?"

"Trying to have a little fun," I said.

"Get back in here!"

We trodded in. Ruddiness looked fine in the ivory cheeks of the Jefferson sisters; the same ruddiness only inflamed Monica's already-red skin. I checked Facebook, as one does after a five minute absence from one's phone. The

pic of Regan and I had been Liked by Dan Good on Regan's wall, but remained unLiked by anyone on my wall.

31

There may be no drug experience as impactful to a person's worldview as initial inhalations of marijuana. At St. Michael's Collegiate weed-smoking was the province of 'scums,' those who smoked by the train tracks and always smelled of cigarettes, those who paid in the oiliest change, and aspired to Truck-centric profile pics. There was a total lack of rebellion among the upper tiers of L-S-C's social hierarchy. We only wanted to be like our teachers and parents, drinking beers at a Triple A hockey game or playing men's league soccer, towing the line. The best compliment was to be thought, "A good guy."

I was at the East Ender with Archambeault and a dozen others the summer after high school ended. I headed outside to engage in an illicit 'session' with some other nascent pot-smokers. It would have been the third time I'd smoked weed, and the first time in a public setting.

Back in the bar I experienced a drastic shift in sensory perception, which was normal during those early weed-smoking experiences, but I was also afflicted by an acute sociological awareness of L-S-C's shittiness. I noticed the drunken girls in their excessive makeup, many of whom had never left L-S-C save for the odd trip to an outlet mall. I noticed the muscle-bound males in their tight white shirts slapping each other on the back, cupping each other's balls in some cases, but only as

proof of how impossible gayness was to them. A phrase popped into my mind to describe the place, "The handshake room." It dawned on me that this would be our lives. Seeing the same people night in/out, exchanging the same handshakes. Worst of all, I wouldn't even rank high on the handshake hierarchy. I'd be scrambling to get better handshakes for the rest of my days. I wanted to share these observations with someone, and began shouting the words, "Handshake room" at Archambeault, who was not keen on his own perceptions of L-S-C being called into question. Archambeault's great spiritual advantage over me was his legitimate happiness in the handshake room.

Rebellion became like a biological imperative. I got on the empty dance floor and did what might be described as an interpretive dance, also accurate would be "aggressive thrusting." Looks were issued. Murmurs heard. L-S-C is as desperate for pariahs as it is for villains. I continued. Some who wished me no ill-will offered weak smiles. Archambeault approached and told me to sit down, but when I wouldn't he left me on that dance floor, recognizing a sinking ship when he saw one.

What sealed my fate was when a pretty girl a few years older than us, who never would have talked to me or known my name otherwise, who must have dug my dance of rebellion at the handshake room, began dancing with me, and even briefly making out with me. So when I returned to the table my attitude was one of, "See, the rules of the handshake room and L-S-C need not be followed. Perpetrate the lies no longer. We can be free of this." No one spoke to me.

I hadn't noticed Dan Good come in with some of the highest-echelon peers he was always so desperate to impress. He always hated when I tried to chew off a piece of his time around these peers, so I went and stood beside him until he became visibly uncomfortable.

"You can relax," I said.

"What?" he asked.

"These people. L-S-C. All this hockey. It's an empty package."

"You're crazy," he said.

I held my middle finger in his face for sixteen quite a fewseconds. It would be the last interaction between us.

32

I tried to engage in some low-level frottage between Monica and Regan on the couch, but the fates were aligned against frottage. We watched a bit of a Dennis Hopper marathon on TBS Superstation. They really pulled out the gems—*The Last Movie, The American Friend,* and *Texas Chainsaw Massacre Part 2.*

I suggested a game of *Trivial Pursuit,* figuring it might bring the household together while allowing me to show off my breadth of general knowledge. Everyone agreed, but my mom had left the game at a nursing home she sometimes volunteered at, so we were forced to play the similar *Isaac Asimov's Super Quiz* instead. Our copy was from 1987, giving a huge advantage to Gary and my mom because they had been alive longer. It was the girls and me v. Gary and my mom. It soon became clear that none of the girls were going to be answering questions about Expo 67 or rocket fuel pioneer and occultist Jack Parsons. It also became clear that my mom was kind of spaced out. It became a heated showdown between Gary and me. Whenever Gary gloated I pointed out his inherent age advantage. He pointed out that I should have bridged that gap from years of having "nose always stuck in a book," which led into our long-running exercise argu-

ment. I felt vulnerable now that my own secret exercise regimen was exposed, but wanted to trust the girls.

"He exercises in secret," said Monica.

"This changes everything," said Gary, unable to contain his glee.

I buried my head in my hands.

"Do you guys have *Operation*? That's what we like to play at home," said Emerald.

A brick was hurled through the living room window, closely followed by the Angered physical self of Mrs. Robertson. Gary employed an economy of movement in getting to his gun and blasting Margaret Robertson into about sixty different pieces all over the white carpet.

"I can't take it anymore!" my mom screamed.

But there was nothing to do besides pick up the pieces of Mrs. Robertson, put them in a garbage bag, Oxy-clean the hell out of the carpet and then dump her nude bod beside Ken String's under the back porch.

"There are bodies under there?" Emerald said. "You should have told me before we played Frisbee."

"Sorry Emerald," I said, giving her a kind of half-hug that prompted every other person in the household to shoot me one collective hate-filled look.

33

That night before the voyage to the sleepytown my mom laid out sleeping bags and blankets for the Jefferson sisters. The girls changed into pajamas and looked adorable.

A worrying noise woke me. Shot, reload, shot. Monica, my mom and I met in the upstairs hallway. I armed myself with the globe mace and crept towards the living room.

Gary stood, autonomic, shooting perfect bulls' eyes dead centre in a painting of a boat that hung on the living room wall.

I should have been more alarmed, but over the years Gary had occasionally experienced waking dreams. One time he'd stood in the kitchen saluting the fridge. Another time he'd picked up Pierre, was carrying him around, patting him on the back and saying, "I've got to burp the baby." That was so funny we let it go on for almost ten minutes. When we woke him he was always disoriented and confused.

In between reloads I tapped his shoulder. "Gary, wake up, you are shooting at the wall."

He looked blankly at all the bulls-eyes in the boat painting, and said, "Oh man."

My mom hauled him back to their room saying, "You know my brother painted that painting."

Later I felt a moment of concern, like, "How did I know this wasn't the deadly manifestation of Gary's Anger." But that passed soon enough and I congratulated myself on my sterling instincts.

The sisters, unaware of Gary's night terror history, clung to each other in the sub-basement.

"Lloyd, what's happening?" asked Regan.

"Only some intruders that I took care of handily."

"Oh my god, Lloyd, you saved us again," she said.

"Actually, I'm just kidding. Gary sometimes has night terrors. He was having one where he was firing a gun at a painting."

"That's scary. What if he shoots one of us next time?"

"His night terrors are like a twice-a-decade phenomenon. It's cool now."

Emerald shivered in the corner, and might have felt left out, so I motioned her over and enjoyed that three-way embrace for about twenty-five seconds before Emerald appeared uncomfortable and wiggled out of the embrace.

Back in my bedroom Monica asked, "What were you doing down there for so long?"

"Comforting them," I said.

34

After the confusion died down everyone went back to sleep. Because I could not sleep I took advantage of Monica sleeping to put my hand on her butt. This provided little solace however. The alarm clock read 2:39. Then it read nothing at all. Another outage.

I went to the fridge and put our three trays of ice into the cooler and then packed proteins among too few cubes.

The other houses in the neighbourhood were also without power. Down the street the team of engineers were hacking into a Hydro box with an axe. I considered taking a shot at them, but knew that Hydro box didn't serve our house anyway, and that our box had already been cut.

I turned the tap. A little poured out and then nothing. I crept past the sleeping Jeffersons. In the sub-basement I found our five gallon jug of stale water. I filled a 1.5 L water bottle and drank the whole thing, giving me a hydration advantage over the household. The next morning I could either maintain that advantage by drinking an equal amount

of water as each household member, or appear magnanimous by drinking less.

Having taken care of everything on Gary's recently-minted outage check-list, I let the household sleep. There'd be enough hysteria and cowering come morning, when at least we wouldn't have to cower by candlelight.

I took a minute to admire Regan's sleeping face. How soft and lamb-y her features were at rest. I wondered what fate had in store for that perfect face. What would it be like to see Regan ice-picked or hacked up by some engineer or as-yet-unknown Angry entity, to see Monica and Emerald's bodies piled in a heap, or to maybe see none of it at all, to be the first slaughtered and hear them screaming, "No, Lloyd, we have always loved you and seen you as exceptional."

Regan woke up. "Now what are you doing?" she asked.

"Another outage," I replied, "Taking care of the items on Gary's checklist. Don't worry. They've been taken care of now."

She drank from a cup of water she had.

"The water is out too," I said, "So you might want to conserve that."

"I'm thirsty," she said.

"Well, drink it now, as it was poured pre-outage, but come morning we're going to have to ration our five remaining gallons."

This reminded me that Monica also had a bedside glass of water that I might purloin.

"Come lie down with me for a minute Lloyd," Regan said.

I did. She put her head on my shoulder and cried quietly so as not to wake Emerald. I stroked her perfect hair, which had always reminded me of the hair of an exquisite horse. I kissed the big puffy crescent of her upper lip. She put her bottom lip on my upper lip. To this end the Anger seemed a boon to me.

"Not here Lloyd," she said.

"Where?" I asked, too eager. "In the sub-basement? On the deck?"

"No, not there either. You better go back upstairs."

"Fuck, fine," I said, not quite gallant, and went upstairs to drink 2/3rds of Monica's bedside water.

35

The smell of frying bacon woke us.

"Good morning Lloyd," said Monica, sounding like she might be on the road to forgiving me.

"The power is out again. Let's go eat our bacon before Gary eats it all."

No side dishes were provided with the bacon. Gary had chosen to heat our last package of crappy old Spalding bacon over the Coleman stove rather than use the high-end stuff from the Jefferson residence. Making matters worse, bacon's saltiness brought to light the water shortages.

"I'm thinking 500 mls of water a day," said Gary. "Believe the human body needs more, but since we are hydrated now, we might be able to last. Then there is the water in the toilet tanks."

"I'm not drinking from a toilet," said Emerald.

"Then you'll die of dehydration," said Gary.

"Calm down Gary," my mom said.

"She might as well get used to the reality of the situation. It's from the tank Emerald, not the bowl," Gary said.

We each got about an ounce of orange juice. Better to have had no orange juice at all, because that ounce was a horrible tease, especially given the saltiness of the bacon and the horrid warmth of the two ounces of water Gary had poured for each of us.

"This small amount of orange juice is almost not worth it," I said.

"I'll drink yours," said Regan.

"No one is drinking anyone's orange juice," my mom said.

After breakfast we wiped grease off our plates with napkins, and then realized we had nothing to wash dishes with, and should have just eaten our bacon directly from the pan. This led to a big argument between my mom and Gary that the rest of us observed awkwardly.

"What should we do now?" Regan asked.

"Read or do whatever vision-requiring activities you might want to do. We have very few candles for when it gets dark," I said.

"We had, like, so many candles at our house," said Emerald.

"So sorry Emerald that I didn't think of every single detail as I was risking my life to rescue you!"

"You were risking your life to use Regan's body!" she accused.

Monica was laughing. Later I asked her what was so funny.

"I saw those posts. You were risking your life for a butt fingering."

36

The girls and I wanted to go outside for more Frisbee during the daylight hours, seeing as there was nothing else to do,

but Gary put the kibosh on that, really undermining my leadership position.

We sat around. The Jeffersons used their phones with reckless frequency. The first and only effort I made to encourage conservative phone use fell on deaf, downright hostile ears.

As spring light faded we sat around the candle as the household had done before Monica's arrival. No one was interested in Sudoku any longer. Still, despite circumstances, there was a pleasant rustic feel. End times could really focus you in on small pleasures like candlelight.

"Is that trembling cry a song?" my mom asked.

"What trembling cry is that?" asked Gary.

"I don't hear a trembling cry," said Regan.

"The invisible worm that flies in the night. In the haling storm?" my mom said.

"No," said Gary, "Not haling."

"What the hammer, what the chain, in what furnace was thy brain? What the anvil. What dead grasp. Dare its deadly terrors clasp?"

"It's William Blake," I said, recognizing lines of verse from Blake's best-known poem *The Tyger*, as any even quasi-literate person would.

My mom left the room. We all exchanged nervous glances. I smelled the smoke of a recently extinguished scented candle, and the contrast of pleasant scent against the dawning madness of my mom made me angry.

"Sunflowers weary of time!" she cried, and held up a long serrated bread knife.

Gary disarmed her with an effective chop-maneuver to the wrist. Then he put her in a full nelson. She kicked and flailed.

"Grab her legs Lloyd," Gary instructed.

I was leery of doing this. She was my mother after all. But the knife-raise spoke for itself. As I reached for a leg she kicked me in the left testicle. As I crumpled to the ground and gasped for breath, Monica took over and grabbed her legs.

"To my workshop!" Gary ordered.

"What?" asked Monica.

"My workshop!"

"Where is that?" she asked.

"It's the sub-basement," I groaned out. For some reason Gary insisted on calling the left side of the sub-basement his workshop, although few tools were kept there and all other household members considered it a storage place.

Monica looked reticent at the top of the steep stairs, which were concrete with a half inch of carpet over them at most.

"Turn this ship around," Gary said, "I'll back down the stairs."

My mom flailed to the extent that I was sure she'd send Gary tumbling to his death, but slowly they reached the halfway point. Having recovered my breath, I said, "Let me take over Monica's position."

"Let her finish the job," Gary said.

I once again felt disenfranchised.

"And what shoulder, and what art..." said my mom.

The Jefferson girls watched from the top of the stairs. Our procession made it to the sub-basement. Gary planned to strap her to a card table. The flimsiness of the card table's legs concerned me. The issue was holding down the flailing woman without the legs giving out. It took the four of us. Once she lost her will to fight, Gary duct-taped her to the table. I asked if there was not a more humane way.

"Sorry Lloyd, I am not a knot expert. Are you a knot expert?"

"I guess not."

Once thoroughly strapped my mother growled, "Damn these mind-forged manacles!"

Later, I went down and tried to give my mother her water, but she wouldn't open her lips. I tried pouring it on her lips a little but that didn't work. I poured some on a washcloth and then dabbed the lips like I'd seen nurses doing on television, which I now realize only works if the person is severely dehydrated in the first place and the lips absorb the water like a plant. In my mom's case the moisture just ran down her chin. Like many mother-dependent young men, I've always had a Proustian soft spot for my mother's well-being, and I had to stifle a whimper.

"Thank you Lloyd," she said as I hunched next to her. "It won't be long now. Muted fear brings peace."

"I love you mom," I said.

"You brought this on us with lust Lloyd. The sexes sprang from shame and pride."

37

With little left to be said after my mom's descent into the Anger we decided to retire to bed early at 8:30 pm. Maybe we believed that in slumber no Anger could invade our hearts.

The Jeffersons didn't want to sleep downstairs for fear that my mom would escape her bondage and attack them with both Blakean invective and physical violence and so we moved their sleeping bags to the living room. Our remaining ounces of water for the day were allotted to us and we all went to bed.

Monica clung to me.

"I'm sorry for everything Monica," I said.

"I know," she said.

"I love you," I said.

"I love you," she said.

When she fell asleep I masturbated to yearbook photos to take my mind off circumstances, and then afterwards felt the worst post-masturbatory guilt I could recall having experienced.

A mewling could be heard through the floorboards. I went downstairs and attended to my mother with a washcloth.

"Trouble wilder and forlorn," she said, "Dark benighted travel worn."

"It's okay mom," I said.

"I told it not. My wrath did grow."

"Don't I know it," I said, trying to bring some mirth into the equation via irreverence.

I dabbed at her lips until she again bore her teeth at me and I decided that was enough dabbing.

In the fridge I found a juicebox hidden behind a box of baking soda and drank it. Its sugar only heightened my thirst. I sang my own in-head song of Innocence and Experience, opened the door quietly and breathed in the air that had been the main air I'd known in my life. I had smelled air elsewhere, but this was my air. I lay in the cold wet grass. My grass. The main grass I'd ever know. I imagined someone in the Serengeti doing the same thing with their own familiar grass. I went back to my room, got my old Sega down from a shelf and had it half set up, hoping to play one last game of Sonic the Hedgehog, which I had loved in youth, before I remembered that the power was out. I looked at Sonic's face on the box, his white-gloved hand on his hip and the other wagging at me like he hated me for all that I'd done. .

"Goodbye Sonic," I said. Would there be another Sonic in whatever lay ahead? Would Mario and old green Luigi be there? Would there be Archies, and Jugheads? For these figures to disappear altogether seemed cruel.

In the living room I observed the Jeffersons. Regan was in my grandmother's old rocking chair, rocking.

"Let's go outside. Get that whiskey," she said.

"I don't want to go down there again."

She got the whiskey while I retrieved tumblers from the kitchen cabinet. We laid her sleeping bag on the deck. We looked at the stars and breathed in the good Lac-Sainte-Catherine air.

"Goodbye to Sonic," I said again, "Goodbye stars."

"Who is Sonic?" she asked.

"The hedgehog," I said.

"I don't like whiskey," she said.

"Who does?"

"Old men do. My dad did."

"They're faking it because it's considered refined," I said.

"Maybe."

"What kind of music did you like?"

"All kinds," Regan said, the consummate non-music lover's answer.

"I liked Bob Dylan. And classical."

"Why did you say it past-tense?"

"We're not listening to music anymore."

I took a two-ounce gulp of whiskey and got on top of her. My lip was bit and ended up bleeding; our teeth banged together a couple times. I lifted her hooded sweatshirt and American Apparel long-sleeved t-shirt, and then fumbled at her bra until she removed it herself. I removed my pants and underwear in a graceless way. Her breasts were inferior to Monica's both in size and shape. It really had been the expensive bras all along. We rubbed at each other leading to my insertion effort. It wasn't long before awkward positioning and flaccidity ruined the moment.

"Want to try again?" she asked.

One positive trait of mine has always been that of per-

sistence. As I was getting close she said, "Wait, do you have a condom?" and I said, "Monica is on birth control," which was not particularly germane, and altogether too much information, bringing Monica into the equation like that.

"Try to pull out," she said.

I failed to pull out.

"Lloyd! You don't think we could be here for a month? For three months? Then I am pregnant and all Monica will do is give me cross-eyed glances. Thanks a lot. Fucking Lloyd."

"If we are around three months from now pregnancy will be the least of our worries," I said, "I'll get you a towel."

She made a sound to indicate displeasure in its purest form. I opened the door softly and came back with a dish towel. After, I threw the soiled towel under the deck beside Pierre and Ken String, whose corpses I had put out of mind and we couldn't smell because of the nice breeze blowing in the other direction.

We sat quietly for a while, I resumed drinking, and the bad feeling from the ejaculation waned. She lay in my arms, needing comfort more than she needed to resent me. I noticed one of the engineers perched on the roof of the String household, observing.

"Let's go inside," I said.

38

Monica was sitting up in bed.

"This is why no one likes you," she said.

She insisted I sleep on the floor, citing body fluids I'd been exposed to and her not wanting those fluids up on her.

As I often did before sleep, I remembered a bunch

of things unwillingly, schemas opening and flowering like poison milkweed. Like the time when Dan Good and I were on a camping trip with Gary, who'd brought a CD of the Grateful Dead's greatest hits. Both Dan and I were like LCD Soundsystem fans at the time for some reason, and based on the name, had always assumed the Dead were a metal band.

"I wasn't expecting this to be so mellow. I thought it would be like, you know, somber," Dan had said.

"I feel super mellow right now," Gary had said. We laughed because Gary had this intense enthusiasm for the Dead that he was trying to pass on to us.

While golfing on that trip, Gary hit a rare green in regulation and we'd insisted he thank the devil. He had refused, but eventually said, "Thank you Satan," and we rolled on the tee-box grass laughing and glowing with the gold of sunshine.

"It's a hand-me down. The thoughts are broken" was a lyric that came to me on my bedroom floor then.

"Monica…" I said.

"Do not talk to me."

I tossed and turned for another hour and then walked around the house. My mom was asleep downstairs, talking in her sleep, saying, "Lured with the smell of infant blood," and then raving about a night-hag.

I went to the kitchen, checked the fridge again, but found no more hidden juices. I debated sneaking more water from the five-gallon jug, but the better angels of my nature won out over hydration greed.

A sleepy-eyed Emerald emerged from the living room in short shorts and the tank top that would have been a bra if it didn't have the stomach-covering part.

"Hi Lloyd," she said.

I looked out the window and saw the engineers running wires around the Robertson home, strapping up what looked to be good old fashioned red sticks of dynamite, all but stamped with the Acme brand of cartoon notoriety.

"What's going on?" Emerald asked.

"Looks like the engineers are blowing up the Robertson' house."

"What engineers?"

"Some Chinese dudes, from out of town I guess. Unless they are some occult manifestation. You see them right?"

"Yep."

"Good. I was beginning to wonder if they were a delusion afflicting me only."

"No, there they are, strapping up dynamite."

"I saw a bunch of travelling circuses on the way to your house. That seemed like it was a delusion because they weren't there on the way back."

"I hope you don't become Angry next," Emerald said.

"Me too. I mean, I hope the same for you, that you don't become Angry."

I patted her back in what I considered a platonic, avuncular fashion. She leaned into me. "Lloyd…I don't want to die a virgin."

"Oh boy," I said, "I'm in pretty hot water with Monica as it is. But don't think it isn't tempting."

"I am not dying a virgin," she said, "If only I'd let Matthew do it when he wanted to last Christmas."

"Ya, that would have been better."

"Is it as amazing as everyone says?"

"Ever see a monkey or a dog do it?"

"Sort of."

"It's like that. One animal thrusting at another animal."

"But it must feel good."

"It feels alright."

"Will you meet me tomorrow night at 3 am when everyone's asleep?"

"I'd better not."

"Fine, then I'm going for Gary."

"Emerald that is sick."

"Why were you really coming to our house?"

"I will meet you at 3 then, but I'm not promising anything."

"You know I can hear everything you guys are saying," Regan yelled from the living room. I scrunched up my face in a way that made Emerald laugh.

Then the Robertson's house blew up. RIP any remaining Robertsons in the house. Gary and Monica came running to the kitchen to ask what happened.

"Engineers blew up the Robertsons," Emerald said complacently.

"What engineers?"

"Some engineers I've been seeing," I said.

"Why didn't you tell me about engineers?" Gary demanded, "From now on tell me everything you know."

The Robertson home burned bright. The wind blew westward so the fire didn't head our way.

"Fierce as ten furies, terrible as hell!" my mom yelled from the basement, must have really screamed actually, for us to have heard her.

"Maybe we should tape her mouth," Regan said.

"Would you tape your own mother's mouth?" I asked.

The Overture from *2001* began playing, if not the world over, then at least in our neighbourhood. It was not amplified from any car stereo. It sounded like it came from on high.

"Great, now some creepy music playing from the sky," Monica said.

"That is the Overture to *2001*," I scolded, "You should know. We just frigging watched it."

"Really Lloyd, what does it matter?" Gary said.

"Ya Lloyd, don't be such a goddamn idiot all the time," Monica said.

Regan laughed.

"Great, now everyone is against me," I said.

"Not me," Emerald said sweetly. Regan and Monica made eye contact and there was this mix of rage and distaste, but also a bit of "What are we gonna do with this guy"/"That Lloyd is incorrigible."/"This is so ridiculous how can we not laugh," and they both smiled rueful so I threw my hands up in the air in a demonstration of conscious incorrigibility and we all laughed except Gary who didn't find any of it funny.

Regan hip-checked Gary in a flirtatious way, indicating all bets were off in terms of social norms, sexual mores, and etc.

39

Gary made small talk during breakfast to distract us from the creep-out of the Overture, but no one wanted to hear about his bygone adolescent interest in falconry. After breakfast Gary enlisted the girls in a brief weapons tutorial, which really should have been given when they first arrived. They took turns swinging the mace globe, aiming the guns, twirling the hockey stick with the knives.

Regan motioned for me to come upstairs so we could speak in private.

"I heard your conversation last night. I'm okay with it. You don't need to hide anything. I bring it up because if it's going to happen anyway, I want it to be nice for her. Because with you and me, it wasn't really..."

"Listen please. I had engaged in onanism mere minutes before that encounter, hence the initial flaccidity."

"What's onanism?"

"Take a wild guess."

"Eww."

The tension was palpable throughout the rest of the day. Monica must have known what was going on. Normally, to relieve tension of such palp, I'd engage in onanistic recreation, but Regan's anti-E.D. warning loomed large. I tried to consider how thrilled I'd have been with this sudden embarrassment of sexual riches only a few weeks earlier.

After a few restless hours of pretending to sleep on the floor, the old watch I'd found in my mom's room finally read 3 am. As I rose from the floor, Monica said, "I know where you're going."

"Sorry," I said.

"Don't apologize for something you're about to go do. You can either do it or not do it. You can't say you're sorry in advance."

"Think about it from her perspective."

"I cannot even believe this. I would have been better off in that trunk," Monica said.

Emerald had laid down her sleeping bag on the deck, and to my surprise, sprinkled dried rose petals she must have brought from home. Her phone was on Power Saver mode, nearly out of even Power Saver power, playing the song *Such Great Heights* by The Postal Service.

I stroked her nice horse hair. We disrobed. She must have thought it was like movies where people kiss with fiery

need and two seconds later they've somehow fallen into each other, but I needed encouragement, which she failed to provide, so I had to encourage myself, which always looks (and is) gross and ape-like. She needed similar encouragement, so I did my best but the sounds of pleasure she made sounded fake. My eventual jam-in effort proved ineffective.

"Can you guide it in?" I asked.

"You don't know how?" asked Emerald.

"I know how. It'll be easier if you help is all."

She tried, but it did not go smoothly and I needed to re-encourage myself for a while and then needed to re-encourage her for a while and certainly things were not off to a roaring start. When finally in, she said, "Ow, Ow," and "I don't think it's in right."

"It is," I said, lost enthusiasm, re-enthused myself, and eventually got it in again.

"Is this it? Are we doing it?" asked Emerald.

"Yep, stop talking please."

"How long do we have to do it for until it counts?"

"Typically until ejaculation," I said.

"What if I don't ejaculate?"

"Typically only the male ejaculates. Or at least a female ejaculation is not something that's guaranteed or ever all that probable," I said.

"This must count by now. You can stop any time."

The next time I needed to be re-enthused I gave up. Sensing my self-consciousness, she said, "It was fine. How's your battery life?"

"Dead," I lied, fearing she'd ask to borrow my phone when hers died.

Too ashamed to rejoin Monica in the bedroom I slept on the downstairs couch, where I could hear my mom yelling, "His dark secret love does thy life destroy" and "O Rose

Thou Art Sick," and stuff about invisible worms. A fitting end to another bullshit night in impotence/shame city.

40

As residents of impotence/shame city often do during their darkest hours, I decided to check Facebook on my phone. It was the usual litany of horrors. For reasons so self-involved, needy and desperate that I will not address them here, I had two Facebook accounts. When I logged into the second I saw a post that was not available to me on the first.

Regan Jefferson: After a brief hiatus we are once again open for business. And by business we mean bod-usage. Emerald still fluffing, Regan still providing butt-fingerings as needed. Come one come all. Angries welcome. We are now at the MacDonald home which is located at [address].

J.P. Scalipi, whom I had fended off at the Jefferson compound, had Liked the post and commented, "Is it legit this time?"

The .22 entered the living room with me behind it. The girls were whispering like snakes. Emerald's eyes rolled back and her tongue shot out and hissed at me.

"Why?" I asked Regan.

"Why not?" she responded.

"You could have killed us while we slept," I said.

"This was more fun," said Emerald.

"Fuck you so hilariously hard," I said.

"Lloyd would have a hard time with that, I imagine," Regan said to Emerald, giggling poisonously.

"Give me your phone," I said.

She didn't move. I jabbed her temple with the barrel of the gun. She handed it over. I did some scrolling. A private message to J.P. claimed she again needed rescue, and would reward him commensurately. Detailed instructions on how to take out the MacDonalds + Monica followed.

I frowned. Emerald retrieved and wielded the hockey/knife-stick from beneath the couch. I sent her out of the game. RIP Emerald.

Regan said, "Think about Dennis Hopper a little bit, Lloyd,"

"Nah," I said, and then her head was all over the place. RIP Regan.

Having become acclimated to killing by this point, I was actually doing the old 'all in a day's work'-style dusting of the hands like an 80s action film hero when Gary and Monica arrived in the kitchen. I lowered the gun and said, "I'm not Angry" with some urgency.

"They were Angry?" asked Gary.

"Yes, and worst of all, probably running some long-con on us from the start. Her brothers may never have been Angry to begin with."

Through the living room window I noticed headlights. I peeled back the curtains and saw J.P. Scalipi getting out of his dad's car down the block, and creep crappily towards us with minimal stealth, though he was definitely aiming for stealth.

Though he wasn't necessarily Angry, and though he was looking for the very bod-use I'd once coveted, I opened the door a crack, and as he crested our curb and encroached upon our lawn, I aimed, sniffed, and sent him out of the game on general principles. RIP J.P. Scalipi.

"That's what I'd call a nice shot," said Gary.

"Thanks Gary," I said.

41

Monica started screaming and crying. Gary and I exchanged a quick glance = 'Angry?' but then through slight eye movements we reached an agreement of 'Probably upset by so many people killed in and around the household is all.'

Gary and I got to work. I grabbed Regan's legs, not wanting to hold the arms, so close to the still-dripping head area. With his combat experience Gary was better suited for that. We struggled to fit Regan's bones and remaining flesh under the deck because Ken String, Mrs. Robertson, and poor Pierre clogged all the available space. We kicked at Mrs. Robertson hoping she would send the rest of the corpses tumbling down the minor slope beneath the deck, but she didn't, so I had to lie down and press my legs against Mrs. Robertson not unlike using the leg press at the gym I secretly went to in the days preceding the Anger outbreak.

"Keep doing those leg-press movements," Gary said, "I can drag the other ones out here on my own."

Leg-pressing Mrs. Robertson in hopes of a corpse cascade, I noticed the engineers again on the String household's roof.

"Really piling up the corpses over there," their leader said. "We could have told you those girls were no good."

"Why didn't you?"

"You didn't ask."

"Any advice for me now?"

"Not really. The end is near enough."

"You guys planning on harming us?"

"No."

"Who are you guys?"

"Just some guys, and the one girl."

"Nice talking to you then," I said, wanting to keep good relations intact with the engineers.

"You bet. Want us to remove J.P. Scalipi's body for you?"

"How do you know his name?"

"We know many things."

"Right. Stuff him under the deck once we're inside please. I'm not sure Gary will take well to you guys. I mean people," I said, nodding at the girl, who, because of androgynous features and short-hair, I had thought was a guy.

"We'll scram then. We'll blow him up with dynamite though. That's what we enjoy doing," said the leader.

They descended from the roof to the opposite side of the String home where they could not be seen. A big rock or something must have dislodged from my leg-pressing because the Mrs. Robertson/Ken String/Pierre pileup finally tumbled downward as I'd hoped it would.

Gary dragged out Emerald's corpse by the feet, leaving a trail of blood and brains that would have to be Oxy-Cleaned later. Through a series of kicks she was added to the corpse pile.

"Lloyd, I've been thinking we get ourselves out of this mess. You know what I mean?" said Gary.

"What if suicides go to hell?" I asked.

"This is hell."

"But maybe by waiting it out we end up in heaven, or at least not hell, but by suiciding it's more of this for eternity, only in a sulphur pit. So far we have it relatively good, with deaths, and weirdness, and shortages, sure, but at least games of Super Quiz and no sulphur."

"What about your mother? Don't we have some obligation to her?"

"Maybe she isn't having that bad of a time. Why not make a nice dinner tonight, a real blow out. To raise our spirits," I suggested.

"Seems ghoulish. I propose subsistence-level dining."

The silence that followed was made no less awkward by the Overture continuing to drone on.

I knocked on the door of my bedroom.

"Go away," Monica said.

"I know you're upset Monica, but we're debating having a big dinner to take our mind off things, and maybe celebrate a little before the coming end," which I immediately regretted saying because it wasn't very cheerful.

"I'm staying in here because I don't trust you," she said.

"Come on Monica."

"How do I know you didn't kill them because you couldn't get a boner?"

"I did not kill them because I couldn't get a boner."

"I listened through the bathroom window. It sounded like you couldn't get a boner."

"Boner-or-no-boner, they were Angered in a strange way. You can check the messages on Regan's phone."

She went silent. Gary was looking at me from the kitchen, grossed out by all the boner talk.

42

We heard digging by the deck.

"Zombified corpses I bet," said Gary. But it was only Bobo, the String's Greyhound, digging out of loyalty to Ken String who was buried there. Something about Bobo's giant grin did my heart good.

"Come here Bobo!" I said. The String's had paid me to walk him when they worked late and their kids weren't around. Bobo trotted over and licked my hand. I opened the door to invite him inside.

"Oh no, not another dog," Gary said like a dad on a sitcom. Really Gary was saying it because of the dire death of Pierre and not needing another Angry dog to have to put in a full-nelson, it's just that his sitcom dad thing was his main model for existing in the world.

"He isn't Angry. He's a good boy isn't he?" I said, the first part to Gary and the second part to Bobo. I filled a dish with Pierre's kibble and placed it before the elongated animal. He ate rapidly.

"Monica, come downstairs. Bobo is here."

"Who the hell is Bobo?"

"The String's dog."

She came out slow, her desire for dog companionship trumping her fear that I'd killed out of boner-despair.

When the dog finished eating she patted his head, and then Bobo lay down on Pierre's blanket and sniffed at it. That made me sad because of no more Pierre. Bobo himself looked a little sad as he sniffed. We took turns petting his head.

Monica said, "I have never seen a Greyhound up close before."

I patted her on the shoulder = 'You have accused me of something heinous, and though I am not guilty, I forgive you.'

"We should take him down and show mom. Maybe she'd like that."

In the sub-basement he sniffed at my mom, but then she called him a "starry pole," which was an apt enough description of Bobo. She then snarled at Bobo, so we took him back upstairs. We threw a toy for him to retrieve but Bobo wasn't that type of dog so he lay down on the bed again to mourn for the dead Strings.

When he started panting I asked Gary if we could give him water.

"No way."

"Regan and Emerald's rations?"

"They shouldn't have had rations in the first place. Those are our rations."

"He can have some of mine," Monica said.

"Mine too," I said.

"Fine, he gets one bowl," said Gary.

We watched Bobo slurp up the water. It felt good to be charitable. I felt it was in our best interest to rack up the karmic bonuses as our demise neared.

Monica and I baby-talked at Bobo for the next couple hours while Gary brooded, brandished the mace-globe ruminatively, and strategized. Monica tried scratching Bobo's belly, but he sneezed, his way of saying, "I don't like that."

I stood on the deck, cursing the Overture above us, and noticed the engineers with shovels and surveying equipment in the backyard.

"What are you guys doing?" I asked.

"We're thinking of putting in a pool."

43

Monica let me sleep in my own bed.

I dreamt of Dennis Hopper in a variety of scenarios:

☻ Dennis Hopper crucified in *The Last Movie*.

- Dennis Hopper as King Koopa in the *Super Mario Bros.* movie.
- Dennis Hopper hosting the most controversial episode of *Monday Night Raw* ever filmed: blowjobs given in the front row, rage-metal playing, the audience possessed by the rage in the metal, then Hoppy sitting in the ring with the rage-band talking about Satan, and Hoppy drinks down an entire bottle of Rum they were all supposed to be sharing, vomits blood, and tells the members of the rage band that if they drink his blood vomit Satan will enter them, but the band members are scared because despite their lyrics about destruction and power they are pussies, and then the ring collapses and the ropes are pulled into a pentagram.
- Hoppy at the grave of D.H. Lawrence.
- Hoppy espousing views on light as "an elemental source of power, like a cosmic coal."
- Dennis Hopper delirious on his death bed repeatedly saying, "500 finales."
- Dennis Hopper and I in a bad auto accident, the two of us dying, maintaining consciousness, despite death, and then a state trooper telling us, "It's alright, you can live."
- Dennis Hopper and I snorting amyl nitrates on a train.
- A James Dean pinkie ring exploding on Hoppy's finger and Hoppy turning into James Dean every time he rubbed that ring.
- Me and Hoppy travelling to a conference that's cancelled and then being stuck in the middle of nowhere, but having a sense of adventure about it all.
- Hoppy introducing me to Vincent Price.
- Hoppy, as he was called, confessing to Charlie Rose.

- Me watching the 42-hour cut of *The Last Movie,* and in the dream the whole cut plays, though I only slept for about six hours.
- Hoppy, James Dean and me riding horses and doing horse tricks.
- Some kind of Stevie Nicks subplot.
- Hopper casting Bob Dylan as a chainsaw painter in a film that flops.
- Something to do with ancient weeds.
- Hoppy lit in the shadows, and then turning into Brando.
- A lightning bolt striking directly behind Hoppy, and he does a celebratory war-dance.
- A past-life Hoppy incarnation as victim of the Spanish War.
- Me very lonely throughout, and not getting help from Hoppy or Dan Good with my loneliness.
- Hoppy and I water-skiing on Lake Temagami.
- Hoppy picking up puzzle pieces.
- Hoppy dressed as an Indian at an Indian casino, greeting the patrons.
- Hoppy on set of some dreadful late-career cable show.
- Dan Good, Hoppy and I having big laughs, then Dan Good turns into Jack Nicholson.
- Hoppy salivating on Jodie Foster then Jodie Foster turns out to be Monica.
- Hoppy in court rooms late in his life to tune of Fleetwood Mac's *Don't Stop Thinking About Tomorrow.*
- A montage of Hoppy hoping for better roles.
- Hoppy on *The Daily Show* while me and Dan Good wait in the green room playing $100 games of pass the ace.
- Hoppy running his finger across a rain drop on his car window and making rain art with it.

- ☻ Hoppy setting off a stink bomb with some high school buddies of his.
- ☻ Hoppy on the golf course with Joe Pesci, Dan Good, Archambeault, Bob Dylan and Dean Stockwell and Dean Stockwell is the only one drunk.
- ☻ Hoppy huffing for Lynch and then Lynch is Leena Moran.
- ☻ Hoppy in tall grass.
- ☻ Hoppy in *Hoosiers* spinning drunk on the basketball court, but instead of Gene Hackman coaching the team it is Gary.
- ☻ Hoppy on streets of Taos, over and over.
- ☻ Hopperian crucifixions, over and over.

I woke up during the part about travelling to the conference, and desperately asked Monica, "What city am I supposed to fly to?"

She said, "You aren't flying anywhere, idiot," because by that point she was used to my weird hypnopompic ramblings.

44

In the morning Monica looked like she might budge in terms of my randiness allotment.

"Aren't there better things we could be doing?" she said, "End times upon us like this."

"Like what?"

"I don't know. You're the big screenwriter. Shouldn't we be reading Shakespeare or something?"

"What's your favourite Shakespeare play?" I asked.

"Don't know."

I opened the big 12-pound Complete Works, flipped to *Twelfth Night* and began reading aloud. She interrupted to say, "The thing I hate about Shakespeare movies is when it's in today time but they still speak like old time."

I nodded.

"The thing about Shakespeare," I said after a moment, reaching for her, "Is it all sucks anyway."

"Maybe you'd rather use the bods of those corpses out there."

"What a horrible thing to say. Besides, they suffered explosive decapitation with evisceration of the brain, so that makes their bods, however intact, undesirable," I said, and we laughed.

Then I read a Psalm from the bible that had always struck me as impressively literary, which was:

> The LORD is my shepherd; I shall not want.
>
> He maketh me to lie down in green pastures: he leadeth me beside the still waters.
>
> He restoreth my soul: he leadeth me in the paths of righteousness for his name's sake.
>
> Yea, though I walk through the valley of the shadow of death, I will fear no evil: for thou art with me; thy rod and thy staff they comfort me.
>
> Thou preparest a table before me in the presence of mine enemies: thou anointest my head with oil; my cup runneth over.
>
> Surely goodness and mercy shall follow me all the days of my life: and I will dwell in the house of the LORD for ever.

"That's nice," she said, "I've never read the bible."

"Not even in elementary school?"

"I couldn't go to a catholic school because I wasn't baptized. I guess they don't care as much by high school."

"Are you worried? About not being baptized? Because of the coming end?"

"Should I be?" asked Monica.

"I'd be."

"Geez."

She looked forlorn, destined for the pit, so I suggested maybe Gary or I could do it for her.

"Doesn't it have to be done by a priest?" she asked.

"Maybe under extenuating circumstances it will go through anyway, you know, with God."

"Do you believe in God?"

"I try to," I said.

"Not sure you should be baptizing me then, half-in, half-out like that, or it might not stick. It might make things worse."

We queried Gary on the matter. Gary was also of tepid faith, attending mass on Christmas and Easter with my mom, but not exactly out spreading the Good News.

"Maybe, Gary, because you've been in the military, you have more weight here," I said.

"This is a question of faith, not rank," said Gary.

Gary and I agreed to a competition where we would call God into our hearts, and on the honour system report a number between 1 and 10 on how much of God's presence we felt in our hearts.

With eyes closed I mind-spoke the words, "I invite you into my heart God," and then my consciousness turned white with a rush of extreme positive feeling.

"I'm saying 10," I said.

"You're not just saying that?" asked Gary, "To win?"

"Saw a white light and everything. It was real."

"Good, I was at like a three or four."

We looked it up on my phone. I blessed water, which I felt pretty weird about doing, like maybe despite the light of only seconds ago I was even in that altruistic effort blaspheming and confining my own self to the pit. I asked Monica if she would follow the teachings of Jesus Christ and turn away from everything evil and sinful. She agreed to do both. I made that old sign of the cross on her forehead with holy water. I thought I heard a shift in the Overture from outside but maybe not.

"Oh boy, that looked really healing and beneficial," Gary pointed out, "I almost want you to do me next."

"Better not," I said, "Since you were baptized as a child, the double baptism might erase the first one."

"Tell me then, big expert, what we do with the rest of this holy water?" asked Gary.

"Maybe sprinkle it on Pierre."

"And Ken String," said Gary "Better idea, put some on your mother's lips."

We tried that, but it did not heal her.

45

Monica and I spent the afternoon in my room. When I went down for our hourly water ration at 4 pm Gary was wielding two steak knives.

"What's up with the knives?" I asked.

"I have water-sickened thoughts," he said.

"Come on, Gary, no."

"I do not greet you as Gary, but as a representative of the Knife Rapists'/Face Eaters' Bund."

"You do?"

"We are the knife rapists. We are the eaters of faces."

This time it was not the scent of a scented candle that contrasted our former life against Gary's unfortunate greeting. It was the frill around a dish towel that hung on the stove. How many evenings and mornings had I seen Gary use that to dry a dish, or wipe a spill off the counter. Now he was mentally ill and aligned with some terrible-sounding Bund.

He elbowed my temple. I saw stars. He pulled my pants downwards. I kicked at him, but he effectively warded off the kicks. He pulled my underpants down. The knife slowed as it neared my rectum, perhaps intended to tease the rectum. In the split second before my rectum was knife-penetrated, Monica shot and killed him. RIP Gary.

"I'm sorry," Monica said.

We made eye contact for a while. I would not add Gary's body to the corpse pile, would not leg-press the corpse of the man who'd raised me down by Ron, the Jeffersons, and poor Pierre.

"Let's get out of here," I said.

We blanketed Gary, cooked proteins and ate. The remaining water from the five-gallon jug we poured into smaller bottles and mason jars.

"What about your mom?" asked Monica.

Monica looked decent, like a good human being.

"I don't know. Should we leave her?" I said.

"She'll die of dehydration."

We left her a few mason jars of water, cut the tape off one wrist and ran. She'd either bring the water to her lips and remain contentedly, Blakeanly confined, or she would

escape. What would happen later we couldn't be held responsible for. RIP mom, in a way.

Because he'd been sleeping and his usual docile-self we almost forgot Bobo, but then, feeling responsible for Bobo, returned for him and made him jump in the backseat. When I turned the ignition the car would not start. The leader of the engineers approached. "Sorry Lloyd, we drained the gas out of the CRV because we needed it for a recent project."

I blinked a few times. We set out on foot, with no destination in mind.

"Where should we go?" I asked Monica.

"Brampton?"

"Too far. We'll never make it."

"Back to my house."

"Your step-dad's corpse will be rotting in there."

"I'm sick of that stuff," said Monica.

We headed out of town along the highway—not on the shoulder where we'd be run down by a freewheelin' motorist out for some kills, or found by a member of the Bund only to have our orifices knifed—but through the bush. The foliage grew thicker and at times we practically swung from branch to branch like ill-coordinated apes, with Bobo having an easier time of things. An old female tramp made herself known.

"There is a moon," she said.

"Totally aware of that," I replied.

Bobo barked at her.

"I have a stale brain," the tramp said.

I sent her out of the game and added her water and some hash and a little hash pipe she strangely happened to have on her to our stores.

"That's what Regan would have looked like after a couple decades," I said, and Monica laughed. How nice it remained to make a pretty person laugh.

Part II

Once you've been warned already. This is warning #2. Proceed further and you are 23802189 times more likely to regret having proceeded further. This is just me in good conscience saying, "Hey, maybe not a good idea to proceed further."

Introduction to Part 2

So something that was ceases to be. What happens when something goes into the past? You go outside and the sky is still the sky, but it is not the same sky you saw when you lived before. The same actions of your lungs and tongue are required to laugh, but you are laughing at someone else, or maybe just laughing at the Internet, and it is not the laughter of the past.

I, Lloyd, may seem cavalier for not going into more grief-related detail concerning the deaths of my parents. And that may seem ghoulish, and make the upcoming events distasteful, like going to a strip club the day after a loved one's death because you feel like touching a woman.

But one thing the loss of Dan Good and the whole gang taught me is that remorse is not confined to an instant. It's not a momentary occurrence that fits neatly in between the paragraphs of one's personal narrative.

I miss you all so much.

46

As morning broke we found a brook too cold to romp or swim in, so we instead splashed water on our faces.

Monica's mother had been a botanist. Around the brook Monica pointed out botanical entities.

"There's some common burdock," she said.

"Is there uncommon burdock?"

"Unsure."

She indicated anemone; cylindrical blazing star; early saxifrage; evening lychnis; elecampane; field wormwood; pussytoes (which I snickered at); hairy rock-cress (on the heels of pussytoes, also kind of pornographic-sounding); devil's urn (she said this one spookily;) razor strop fungus; water horehound; crown and cow vetch; shrubby potentilla; creeping snowberry; turkey tail; rose pegonia; reindeer lichen; meadow rue; foam flower and fragrant bedstraw; purple dead-nettle; creeping juniper; bladder campion; clintonia aka blue bead lily; all kinds of dog bane; interrupted fern; spotted Joe-Pye weed; kalm's lobelia; maidenhead spleenwort fern; and orchid of the hellobrine variety. {332087672372202}

"Are all those really in this brook area?" I asked.

"No, only a couple. I said them cause I'm saved now, and it seemed like a fitting tribute to God who made those things, and to my mom who loved them and knew their names."

"That's nice," I said, and we smoked hash, drank a lot of water, and rested on our sleeping bags.

Bobo eyed a squirrel, pounced in its direction. The squirrel was too fast.

"Hey, there really is a moon," Monica said, and though it was morning, the moon shone nearly as bright as the sun, right beside the sun, like a twin devil.

Bobo howled at the moon, and Bobo was not a howling type of dog. I had never even heard him bark. So I howled with him.

"Don't," said Monica, "You'll attract nearby Angries."

47

She was right, a few hours later the idyllic scene was interrupted by an announcement from the Bund.

"We do now declare these acres property of the Knife Rapists'-Face Eaters' Bund. Individuals trespassing hereon will be subjected to vaginal and rectal knife penetrations followed by the chewing off of face flesh. We will not eat your other body parts, let it be known," and then the message repeated, sounding like it was coming over a loudspeaker.

To Bobo's credit, he did not give away our position by barking.

"We better get moving," Monica said. She looked tired.

We grabbed our packsacks and ran in the direction opposite the Bund's announcement, running the first few hun-

dred yards and then slowing to a brisk walk when I became winded. Monica remained unwinded.

"Where to now?" I asked.

"The old Temagami Music Camp isn't far from here," said Monica. "I spent a summer there when I was in the Community Theatre Workshop. They have cabins and things."

It was six kilometres away and took us two hours to reach. An advanced guard of girls from the CTW greeted us. They were a fairly non-intimidating advanced guard of two beautiful actresses I recognized from the Scapino castration video and previous CTW plays I'd seen. Monica knew them from her time in the theatre. Bobo sniffed their palms and seemed to approve.

"And what's your name?" one of the girls asked Bobo in a dog/baby voice.

This always irked me because it was obviously a human responsibility to provide the answer. Sometimes when Pierre was queried in this manner I wouldn't even answer. If I did it was always in a disdainful monotone, but here I wanted to make a good impression, so I kept the disdain out of my voice and put positive inflection on the tone when I said, "Bobo."

"Hi Bobo!" one said.

"Are you guys Angry?" the other asked.

"No, are you?" asked Monica.

"No way. Some people think we are, because of Leena's vision, but we believe Leena is our best hope."

"This is Lloyd. Lloyd this is Ashley and Brianne," Monica said with skepticism = 'Would you use their bods were the opportunity to arise? Probably, given your foul actions of recent weeks.'

"What kind of operation are you running here?" I asked.

"We are making *The Last Movie*, combined with other movies, including *Night Tide, Tracks,* and *Out of the Blue,*" said Ashley.

"What's *The Last Movie*?" Monica asked.

"We just fucking saw it on TV," I almost yelled.

"Okay, relax," Monica said, and I felt bad for embarrassing her in front of her friends.

"Leena thinks only we can give Dennis the tribute he requires. And that doing so may end the Anger."

"The Dennis dreams are universal?" I asked.

"We've all had them," said Ashley.

"What happened to *Eyes Wide Shut*?" I asked.

"We performed it a few times but no one came, then Leena had a dream vision from Dennis himself," said Brianne.

"How's Scapino?" I inquired.

"Not so bad. We're keeping him doped up. His wound was, what is it, cauterized, so he won't bleed to death or anything," said Ashley.

Brianne, the bustier of the two, and thus my immediate fave, said, "You guys should totally join us. We can always use another actress of Monica's caliber, and we are short on young males."

Monica and I exchanged a glance.

"Not to be rude, but just to get this out of the way—how do I know I won't suffer a Scapino-like fate?" I asked.

"One, that was only needed for Leena's vision of *Eyes Wide Shut*, and two—there was some bad blood with Scapino, so he had that coming," said Ashley.

"I don't know," I said.

"We have food and water," said Ashley.

"What about security?" asked Monica.

"Leena reached an agreement with the Bund," said Ashley.

"This Bund has really proliferated quickly," I said.

"The Bund had been laying the foundation for some time," said Brianne.

"What's the deal you have with the Bund?" Monica asked.

"That we'll perform our play for them at a big festival they're planning," said Brianne.

"I envision the other events at that festival would involve heinous amounts of knife-raping and face-eating," I said.

"Yikes," said Ashley, also very cute. "But Leena says that have to deal with whatever arises."

They brought us to the dining hall, introduced us to a few of the other actors, and gave us plates of leftover Salisbury steak. Bobo was given fat from the compost, which he seemed fine with. The power remained on. The fridge was stocked with two months' worth of food for the May-scheduled Regional Classical Music Camp that would never be.

As the co-head of the former MacDonald household I requested a briefing with the operation's leader.

"She only talks to immediate underlings during the day, but she addresses everyone during rehearsals. You can talk to one of the underlings. We are like the 4th and 5th ranked though, so we can tell you anything you need to know," said Brianne.

"What if non-Bund Angries attack?" I asked.

"Most of the Angries in this area are either aligning with the Bund or being taken out by the Bund. Leena offers salvation from Anger," said Ashley.

The girls showed us a small cabin we could occupy. It even had a foam mattress. We laid down our possessions and later the girls came by with a housewarming gift of incense sticks. Monica lit these and gave me a hug. Randiness ensued.

"I should go talk to Scapino," I said afterwards.

48

Monica stayed in the cabin to arrange our sundries and make a bed for Bobo. I found Ashley bent over the stage in the barn, scrubbing the floor.

"I wish to speak to Scapino," I said.

"Scapino is sleeping now. He's heavily medicated."

"Are there lucid periods?"

"Sure."

She gave me a look, and asked if I'd like to see her cabin.

The possibility of sexy results outweighed my castration anxiety. As soon as we'd broached the entrance she disrobed. Her bod was the nicest bod of all the bods described up to this point in the narrative. No Emerald-style difficulties. I was able to get the job done, salving my ego after the Regan/Emerald fiascoes.

"Sorry I didn't pull out," I said after once more failing to do so.

"That's fine. Leena's encouraging us to have offspring."

"That strikes me as disconcerting," I said.

"I'm happy a young guy showed up, since Scapino is, well, poor Scapino."

This seemed at least a temporary guarantee against my own castration.

"Monica has been through a lot," I said, aiming for a tone of gravity appropriate to end times, "I'd prefer if you not mention this to her."

"Brianne wants to be impregnated too," said Ashley.

"Well, I can only do my best."

"You have a mystic power," Ashley told me.

"Thanks, I've always thought that about myself."

"May I take a video of you on my phone?"

"Sure."

"Please say, 'We blew it.'"

"You know that's Peter Fonda's line right?" I asked.

"We are mixing and mashing," said Ashley.

"We blew it," I said with a pathos that I felt conveyed the tragic nadir of late 1960's idealism.

In our cabin Monica sniffed at me.

"You smell like sex."

"Ya, we recently did the handjob/beav-rub combo."

"You smell like a vagina."

"Yes, your vagina."

"Nope, someone else's vagina."

"You're crazy," I said, reminding myself to clean my genitals better after the next go-round with Ashley, Brianne, or whoever else wished to be impregnated.

"I think I know what my own vagina smells like," Monica said.

"Do you?" I asked.

49

We brooded in silence until we heard that dinner bell ring. Bobo, through dog ESP, understood this signified food and his ears perked up.

"I'll bring you something Bobo," I said, to reassure Monica, or perhaps myself, that I was a good man.

The dining hall was set up with long tables like you'd see in a church basement, seating about twenty. I took a moment to size up my competition, which consisted of three old-

er men, seniors, Rotary types, closet admirers of Brianne and Ashley until the impregnation order I suspected; one post-operative male-to-female transgendered Francophone individual, who obviously did not retain the ability to impregnate; one handsome young gay man, who, while able, was presumably unenthusiastic about impregnating the cast of adolescent babes because of being into dudes. I patted this guy on the shoulder because L-S-C is a repressive community, our most common slur is "Gay," and people in our region would say, 'That's gay,' to indicate a soccer field that had grown too muddy to play on, but I was above that, hence the shoulder pat. Also, I liked how his orientation affected this ratio:

> Pretty girls to be impregnated : Lloyd minus Lloyd's competition of guys desiring/realistically able to impregnate pretty girls.

Scapino was of course impregnating no one.

I considered sitting at the old man table to indicate, "Hey, I'm a man here too, happy to engage in lawn-mowing, hammering, or any other masculine tasks needing doing," not out of fealty to those weak old rubes, but to show the girls that yes, there was a potent man's man in this commune. Before I could make any such decision, friends of Monica signaled her over.

"Monica, we're so glad you're back! How long has it been?" one asked.

"Since *Fiddler*," Monica said.

"Wow, I can't believe it. We were just talking about you the other day," said another.

"This is my boyfriend Lloyd," Monica said, looking at me like, 'Please do not humiliate me any more Lloyd.'

"Howdy," I said, and already she seemed humiliated by me.

Dinner was served by a mannish woman in her 60's or possibly 70's. I excluded her from the Lloyd/Chicks Requiring Impregnation (L:CRI) ratio due to her evident lowness of estrogen and concomitant lowness of reproductive possibilities. Dinner was a vegetarian chili lacking in both heartiness and textural appeal.

A woman I recognized from high school entered. She'd always been a capital-A actress, enunciating intensely, singing in difficult pitches in hallways, doing leg lifts for no reason. She had wide hips and a face that shared some properties with Liz Taylor's 1948 face. She would have seemed pretentious were she not genuinely afire with some true searcher's intensity. Her name was Solange Meriwether.

"We are so happy to welcome two new friends into our family. Or one new friend and one old friend," said Solange.

She approached Monica, made Monica stand, and hugged Monica. "I have missed you so much Monica! And who's this handsome fellow?"

"This is Lloyd," Monica said with caution.

I too was made to stand, and was hugged.

"Pleasure to meet you," said Solange.

"We went to high school together," I said.

Solange pretended not to hear. Instead she performed a little pirouette to show how in love with art and life she was.

"Lloyd is a screenwriter," Monica said.

"You are?" asked Solange.

"I've written a few things. Rarely has anything been produced," I said.

The only thing produced was an ode to the St. Michael's Collegiate football team that did not achieve the Mallickian transcendence I'd aimed for, but was more like a collage of photos.

"Amazing," said Solange.

Monica and I weren't sure whether to sit down or remain standing. So I half-sat down, but Monica remained standing, leading me to over-correct mid sit-down and jerk back up. One of the old men snickered.

"Now for the dire news," Solange said, pantomiming direness, "Your jobs! Everyone in the family does something. Hmm, let me see. Lloyd, given your skill set I think you should be on Festival Operations."

Gasps greeted this, suggesting I'd landed a plum gig.

"Monica, since you left us, you'll have to start fresh on the PooPoo/PeePee Battalion," Solange said.

Over a three-second period, Monica's green irises occupied every possible space within her eye sockets.

"Who else is on the battalion?" Monica asked after all the iris activity ceased.

"Mert used to head up the Battalion, but he is moving on to Signage."

Later that night in the cabin, Monica asked me, "What the hell is up with a name like the PooPoo/PeePee Battalion?"

"A sort of ironic thing. Like they are such sophisticated artists they can use juvenile language and because of the many layers of ironic removal it's considered the living end."

"Do you want to stay here?" she asked.

I did. "I don't know. Do you?"

"Depends how things go with Mert tomorrow."

"Mert seems like a good guy," I lied.

When Monica fell asleep I tried to sneak over to Brianne's cabin as per the note she'd slipped me during charades, but Bobo barked and woke Monica, so I said, "Going pee, be right back." And then under my breath said, "Fuck you Bobo."

50

I woke up early and sought out Scapino, creeping around the cabins until I heard a male mewling noise. A gap in his cabin's boards revealed Scapino tied with bed sheets in a standing position.

"Hello Scapino," I said.

"What am I doing here?" he asked.

"You're with the acting group."

"Don't remember anything. Want to be left alone. Don't remember anything after I got on the subway," he said.

"That was a long time ago. There was an accident."

"Can you help me get out of here?" he asked.

"I better not."

"Why is this happening to me?"

"Not sure Scapino, but times are tough all over," I said, somewhat glib in the face of Scapino's madness and dick being gone, so I added, "Can I get you anything?"

"My mind back," Scapino requested.

At our cabin Mert was knocking on the door. Monica eventually got out of bed and followed Mert to the latrines. Bobo jumped on the bed with me and we slept for two hours.

When Monica returned she was an unhappy camper. She described battalion duties thusly, "Cleaning the actual bathroom wasn't so bad. Standard scrubbing, flushing, mopping, and so forth. The septic tank is the real bastard. It gets clogged. You have to reach down inside and unclog it, according to Mert sometimes that unleashes a spray. My face was sprayed."

"Sorry to hear that Monica."

"Weirdest was that, despite being like 100, Mert made a pass at me, and when I mentioned having a boyfriend, he said you'd be busy 'seeding the crops,' and when he said

'seeding the crops' he made air quotation signs with his fingers. Any idea what that's about? Sure was gross."

"Can't say that I do."

She leaned in to kiss me, the usual prompt for the morning's festivities, but as she'd recently been sprayed by septic matter, and I expected to service upwards of three ladies throughout the day, I declined, citing my own morning breath, even though my breath was always quite fresh.

51

Gritty oatmeal greeted us in the dining hall. The screaming meemies of the Overture screamed on. When Monica motioned for me to sit with her I glanced instead in the direction of the gay dude my age who seemed a likely ally. I figured it good optics to branch out and befriend the entire cast, not just potential sex partners.

"Hey," I said, "I'm Lloyd."

"Timothy," said Timothy.

"Seen you in a couple CTW productions. *Joseph*, possibly."

"Yep, I played Joseph. Monica is a great girl."

"Totally agree with you Big Tim. Anyone ever call you Big Tim?"

Big Tim laughed. Off to a good start with Big Tim, I thought.

"So you have a dog?" he asked.

"A Greyhound, Bobo."

"I miss my own dog. Jonathan. I miss my whole family," said Timothy.

"Me too," I said, avoiding the obvious question of, "Dead?"

"Who knows what happened after I got swept up with the CTW. It was all so crazy. The Bund attacked, then Leena successfully negotiated with the Bund, so I figured this was my best option. My parents haven't answered my texts."

"Same position Monica finds herself in," I said.

He leaned and spoke in a near-whisper that Mert and the other geezers at our table couldn't hear, "Did you see what happened to Scapino? Don't take this the wrong way, but I was happy when you showed up, because, now, like, two potent males means my castration is only half as likely to happen. No offense."

"None taken. I was hoping for like a firm no-castration guarantee when I meet with Leena," I said.

"You expect to meet with Leena?"

"I'm on Festival Operations you know."

"You will report to Solange. Be careful what you say," said Timothy.

"What are you young fellas talking about?" asked Mert.

I shot Mert a dirty look = 'I know you have designs on Monica, Mert.'

After breakfast we were led in an apparent every-morning-type Tai Chi routine by Solange. She said things like, "Expel the bad spirits, take in the good," and "Be one with the Bund and creative spirit at once. Feel the Bund energy dissolving into the white."

Instead of doing that I checked out the bods of Brianne, Ashley et al in their tank tops and short shorts. Mert was similarly checking out Monica, so I cleared my throat in the direction of Mert. Interesting how another's lascivious leer is exponentially more horrifying v. one's own.

Bella, the low-E cook, ran from the kitchen, crying, "Flood, flood."

No one knew how to respond for a minute until Solange said, "Monica..." because apparently kitchen floods fell under Battalion

detail. Sensing an opportunity to curry favour with hard-done-by Monica, I offered to help. The pipe beneath the sink, referred to by Bella as a U-Trap, was leaking and needed to be replaced.

"Are there replacement pipes?" Monica asked.

No one had an answer. Eventually we settled on black hockey tape that didn't look like it would hold for long.

"Try not to use much water I guess," said Monica.

"Impossible,"said Bella, "I'm cooking for twenty-five people."

"I don't friggin' know. I'm not a plumber," said Monica, and then Bella filled out some L-S-C CTW grievance report against Monica that both Monica and I scrunched our faces at = 'C'mon Bella, just cause you are low-E and full of hate don't go writing Monica up for dealing with the situation as best she can.'

Solange came in, ignored Bella's complaints, and asked to speak with me. We went to her cabin, I presumed for a briefing on Festival Operations duties, but she too had been commanded to grow a baby. Being a slightly older woman she worked hitherto unknown angles on me, both emotional and physical, and employed techniques that I believe the descriptor of 'tantric' is an apt descriptor of. [50980941100110101010103]

As I caught my breath, she said, "Poor Lloyd, you must be getting tired."

"I'll get by," I said, and then addressed her as "lover," which seemed to gross her right out.

52

Solange told me I wouldn't be needed for a couple hours, so I grabbed a quick nap full of Hopper dreams, highlights including:

- Beautiful, unfinished Hopper films lovingly restored by Paul Schrader and presented at galas.
- An older Hopper networking with doughy Chamber of Commerce members.
- A Peruvian priest de-frocked after Hoppy convinced him to conduct an occult James Dean-focused ceremony.
- Hopper, several years too old, as the lead in *Repo Man* instead of Emilio Estevez.
- Hopper rafting down the Nile.
- Hopper and Scapino in a New Orleans cathedral, with Scapino in post-penile anguish.
- Hopper and me hauling ass down a highway, which was neat.
- Hopper casting Errol Flynn in one of his unfinished masterpieces, and Paul Schrader discussing the importance of this.
- Hopper cheering on a Chickee Run.
- Hopper and Nic Ray sharing Natalie Wood's bod.
- Hopper saying, "I'm the asshole" and pouring booze all over his head.
- A young Hopper heralded as doing the best seizure in the business.
- Hopper accusing Rock Hudson of prejudice, both filially, and filmically.
- Hopper doing Strasbergian exhalations before campaigning for the Republican Party.
- 20-something Hopper as a spectre at The Museum of Modern Art.

Then Monica came in and said, "They need you Lloyd, some guys are here with big motorbikes, guys from the Bund," which I did not like the sound of one bit.

53

When I reached the driveway I saw:

- 🏵 Two late-model Ford F150s, black.
- 🏵 One old green truck, later identified as a 1982 Ford F150
- 🏵 Two motorcycles later identified as 1950 and 1952 Harley Davidson Hydra-Glide Bikes.
- 🏵 Three members of the Bund, one of whom had a face tattoo, and another, whom I didn't get a great look at, could have been the female Engineer.

The Bund members drove off in one of the F150s. The calculus of the situation was apparent. The bikes would be ridden by Captain America and Billy. The remaining Ford F150 would be the shooting vehicle, although any student of cinema knows Laszlo Kovacs used a Chevy comfortable. The older truck would be the truck that the hillbillies shoot Captain America and Billy from at the end of *Easy Rider.*

Solange took charge, "Come here Lloyd. Come here Timothy. Today you two lucky guys begin motorcycle training. Leena mentioned filming the ending of *Easy Rider* for use as a video installation at the festival. Timothy, we're thinking Scapino will play the role of Captain America, so that we can really shoot Scapino dead, but we need you for the B-roll."

"That's fine," Timothy said.

"Lloyd, you'll be playing Billy in both the B-roll and A-roll, but we won't shoot you for real," said Solange.

"But I get to say the line, 'We blew it.'?" I asked.

"Leena will discuss that in rehearsal today."

"Why no rehearsal yesterday?" I asked.

"Leena had a migraine," Solange said, and then added, "Lloyd, have you met Mert? Mert has the most motorcycle riding experience in the company. He will instruct this tutorial."

"Thought Mert was on signage," I said.

Timothy and I mounted choppers. A crowd of curious girls and Mert's two buddies watched. Had they nothing better to be doing? Signs to be made? Accretions of poo and pee to be battled against?

After instructions on how to give it gas, put it in gear, and drop the clutch, Timothy's bike roared to life. I was ineffective in my dropping of the clutch and the bike lurched in a terrifying way, nearly maiming Mert. I stalled the bike several more times before Mert said, "Easy son. Haven't you ever ridden a four-wheeler before?" because four-wheeling was popular among northern Ontario hicks like Mert and his offspring.

"Wasn't really my thing," I replied, "Having led a life of the mind prior to the Anger disease."

I got the hang of it and we took turns riding our choppers down the long driveway and back. Then we did it side-by-side. At one point I collided with Timothy and Timothy crashed to the ground, but due to our slow speed he wasn't injured.

"You boys are going to need practice before we can run this shoot at top-speed," said Mert.

"Eat a dick Mert," I said.

Mert's face dropped. Mert's cronies all shook their heads = 'This Lloyd guy waltzes in here, makes love to all the young women we desire, can't even drop a clutch and is now mouthing off to Mert with no respect for Mert's tenure in the CTW whatsoever.'

Intervening, Solange said, "That's enough for now boys. Our set design people need to paint these bikes."

Ashley and a girl named Penny got to work painting iconic stars and stripes on Captain America's bike. Since Scapino was not there taking the motorcycle training, I figured they planned to simply strap Scapino's catatonic husk to the bike, and maybe tie his foot to the accelerator.

54

After the motorcycle training everyone went their separate ways. Some of the nerdier kids played *Magic: The Gathering*. Monica and a couple of her friends put Sun-In in their hair and sat in the sun hoping it would make their hair blonder. Solange did more tai-chi even though we had already done a lot in the morning.

Four figures walked up the long drive. Two of them were girls from the CTW, on the same sentry duty that Ashley and Brianne had been on when they found us. The other two had potato sacks over their heads.

"Two prisoners," said Candy, armed with a Derringer. Ashley and Brianne must have been similarly armed when they found us, but, having recognized Monica and a fertile male with the characteristics needed to portray youthful Dennis Hopper, did not draw them.

"They say they were released by the Bund," said the other girl, Penny.

"Doesn't sound like the Bund I know," I said, still trying to fit in, "The Bund is more into knifing butts and eating faces. Right? Right guys?"

Sacks removed, I recognized two individuals I'd attended elementary and high school with. The male was Alatragus Pino, a close friend in second through sixth grade, in which grade I'd ascended to unimagined heights of popularity due to my association with Dan Good. Prior to my ascension, Alatragus and I had spent entire school weeks planning sleepovers, scheming to wear underwear on our heads as was seen on sitcoms, to steal bags of chips from his parents and change from mine, to generally engage in all-night hijinks.

The girl was Pino's cousin Jenny Caveat. And please don't think I'm making up funny names in some bid for a post-modern, maximalist tone. It is strictly coincidence that people involved in the events surrounding my end times experience have funny- or zany-sounding names. I would point out the many non-funny names as evidence of name verisimilitude: Gary, Monica, Pierre, Solange (fairly common among Francophones), Ashley, Brianne, Penny, etc. The only funny names being Bobo; Blind Harv; Jenny Caveat; maybe my name of Lloyd is a bit funny, but I can't help that; and maybe Mert is funny-sounding too, but 60 or 70 years ago it would have been normal to name a kid Mert, or whatever the full version of Mert might be. Mertus maybe? As for Alatragus, he was named Alatragus because his father was a denturist.

"Hi Lloyd," said Jenny Caveat, who bore a strong resemblance to the (suicidally-) late photographic genius Francesca Woodman, whom I have sort of befriended in hell.

Jenny Caveat had been the sweetest and kindest girl in our grade. So sweet that whenever a new girl entered our class from elsewhere, the type destined for cruel verbal abuse, our teachers sat them beside Jenny and her best friend Eleanor Von Geng. (Funny, but also real!) While everyone liked Jenny and to a lesser extent Von Geng, the two always had these can-

cerous sorts hanging off them because they were too kind to shake them off. Jenny grew up to be gorgeous, but due to her demure nature, she never garnered the attention of a Regan. We always had a kind word for each other over the years as people who grew up in the same grade tend to.

"Lloyd, hilarious! What are the chances?" Alatragus said.

"We are sooooo happy to see you," said Jenny Caveat, whose face was sweating because she'd had the potato sack over it.

I gave Solange a look as a means of vouching for them.

"If you vouch for them, and it does not go well, it will be your head on the pike," Solange said.

"Alatragus is a fertile young man with no shortage of public speaking experience," I said, "Jenny Caveat here is one of the finest human beings I have known on this too sad earth."

"Are you two in a relationship?" Solange asked them.

"We're cousins," Jenny said.

"Good, then, you, your name?"

"Alatragus."

"Alatragus can help seed…" began Solange.

I cleared my throat, approached Solange, and whispered, "Please keep the seeding talk on the down-low in front of Monica."

Solange frowned and said, "Lloyd will brief you on your responsibilities."

I showed the cousins to an empty cabin near ours.

"How did you escape the Bund?" I asked.

"You'll never believe it," Alatragus said, "Dan Good is the leader, or at least some kind of regional leader, of the Bund."

I tried not to show emotion. Alatragus knew of my falling out with Dan. I knew how it'd always looked to peers like Alatragus. That I was to Dan Good what Sal Minneo was to James Dean in *Rebel Without a Cause*: a toadie, an afflicted worshiper.

"He let you go?" I asked, aiming for a tone of info-exchange between end times tacticians.

"He said we could try our luck here. He washed his hands of us. Like Pontius Pilate," said Alatragus.

"Very much like Pontius Pilate, including some kind of robe," said Jenny.

We all nodded, remembering depictions of Pilate from our Catholic school lessons.

"The Bund killed our family," Jenny said, reminding us that despite motorbike training and games of *Magic: the Gathering* we were in tough times with dead family and friends abundant.

"Are these people crazy?" Alatragus asked.

"Most likely. But crazy in the same way they've always been crazy, which is a cult-like fealty to Leena Moran, and that's a craziness we can deal with. A craziness preferable to that of the Knife Rapists'/Face Eaters' Bund, is my feeling," I said.

I brought Alatragus to the kitchen and opened the freezer door. When Bella shrieked out a complaint I told her it was my right as a member of Festival Operations, which she reluctantly accepted. After scooping potato salad from a big vat, I explained Pino's impregnation duties to him. Despite the recent deaths of his loved ones, Alatragus seemed enthusiastic about the opportunity to bang a lot of mid-to-late adolescents.

55

The dining hall buzzed in anticipation of Leena's appearance. By 4:15 there were murmurs of concern. At 4:27 Solange walked down from Leena's two-story cabin atop the hill

and said, "I'm sorry everyone. Leena has another migraine. Rehearsal is cancelled again."

Groans greeted this, and a few sideways glances = 'How crazy is Leena and is Solange keeping her away from us for a reason, and if so is Solange really the one running this thing?'

"This is boring," said Penny, one of the more petulant young girls, who was desirable except for some kind of eczema issue.

"What should we do?" asked Jeanette.

"Let's play a game!" said Ashley.

"We've already played all the games," said Brianne, pouting.

I'd noticed a pile of worn sports equipment in an enclave near the bathrooms. Hockey sticks, all-purpose rubber balls that are balls of all purposes but effective balls of none, a dented Easton baseball bat, a softball coming apart at the seams, and a half-dozen gloves dating back to the earliest Pierre Trudeau administration.

"How about a game of baseball?" I asked.

Some of the girls made little shows of how fun and cute baseball was. I pictured them falling down, laughing, making a mockery of God's finest game. Still, I was anxious to show off my skills. When enthusiasm reached the point of consensus, I cried, "First captain first pick! Last one to touch that support beam is second captain!"

As any veteran of elementary schools knows, second captain is the worst position, especially if the second captain is himself unskilled. The skilled first captain would select the best player, leaving the second captain with the second best remaining player. The first captain, the most aggressive jerk, was usually skilled. I had never been first captain material prior to taking up with this crowd. Further, it was a rea-

sonable assumption that a second captain under the last-to-touch system would be unathletic because he/she was least expedient in touching something. The last man to reach the support beam was Mert, having had a hard time getting up off the couch.

"Mert's second captain!" Candy yelled scornfully.

"Wait, Bella hasn't touched," Mert's friend Larry said.

"Not playing," Bella said from the kitchen.

In the field behind the cabins we laid down sweatshirts and things for bases. One of the bases was a big cardboard sign that Mert didn't want to use for signage because he had signage material superior to it.

With first pick I chose Alatragus. From previous softball experiences I knew he could solidify first base. With outs hard to come by in co-ed amateur softball, first base was a big deal. At draft's conclusion the teams looked like this:

Team Lloyd:

1B: Alatragus; 2B: Jenny; 3B: Leanne (great looking, but with some kind of limp); SS: Lloyd; Outfield: Candy, Ashley, Brianne, Penny; C: We decided to let the ball roll to the backstop and the batter could throw it back, and the pitcher would cover home plate for plays at the plate, because of little point having a catcher for softball. P: Monica. Manager: Timothy, who chose not to play but still wanted to be involved.

Team Mert:

1B: Lewis Orlovsky (Another high school classmate of mine, but one who suffered about ten concussions too many and was borderline vegetative); 2B: Burt; 3B: Larry SS: Lee (previously mentioned ESL-type older French-Canadian transgendered person living as a woman but not making it easy on anyone with the unisex moniker, solid shortstop it turned out, however) OF: Jeanette, Mert's friend Burt, Solange; P: Mert.

A coin flip designated Team Lloyd the home team. Mert's two older pals were struck out handily by Monica, who'd played girls softball and could put a tough spin on the pitches.

Team Lloyd pointed and laughed at the feeble swings while Solange criticized and encouraged Team Mert from the sidelines. Mert batted himself third as though he was Don Mattingly, but hit a weak grounder to short that I barehanded to show how weak of a grounder it was and then sidearmed to Pino at first. It was maybe the first perfect inning in the history of co-ed softball and an auspicious start for Team Mert.

It started to rain. How good those girls looked in that rain and that sunlight. All just light, I thought. No light, no gleaming droplet on Ashley. No light, no hilarious image of Mert picking his underwear out of his butt on the mound. No light, nothing but old blackness of self. The phrase "Vanessa Hudgens and the varieties of religious experience" popped into my head, so I spoke it to the second baseman Burt after I'd hit a double. Burt winked at me.

In the second inning Larry made a terrific diving grab to rob Monica of at least a triple. Everyone cheered for Larry, who limped up from the ground and smiled. Every ball thrown to Lewis Orlovsky at 1st flew right past him, was not even waved at by Orlovsky, so Team Mert only recorded outs on fly balls. During the third inning stretch Solange wheeled Scapino out to watch. He was zonked out on Oxycontin however and probably perceived little.

The odds of a close game in softball are astronomical, but by pure chance, and a total lack of discipline in the Team Lloyd outfield, the score was 28-28 in the bottom of the 5th. We'd agreed to play only five innings because each inning was taking a solid forty+ minutes.

I was on first when Pino singled to centre. I should have stopped at second, but I tore around second, and then tore

around third as the ball hit the cut-off man. The cut-off man was Burt, which was his real name and not made up for comic effect relative to the name of Mert. Mert covered the plate. The ball arrived before I did. Mert squared for collision. Everything I had went into that collision: every mournful thought of Pierre, Mom and Gary; every guilt for the Reganian fiasco; every guilt for my ongoing betrayals of Monica; every even wayward sad thought for someone like Blind Harv or Ken String; every hatred of the Tumour man; every nostalgic night-ache for Dan Good; every sad hope for the world to get better.

I put all that into the collision and in doing so I separated Mert's shoulder, and also concussed Mert, which no one realized initially, so as the ball squirted out I slapped Monica's sweatshirt/home plate and screamed a cry of exhilaration. My team ran to me, tried to lift me, failed, so we hugged and I lifted some of the girls and Alatragus lifted some of the girls, and I high-fived Jenny, and kissed Monica passionately until it became clear that Mert was going to need medical attention.

56

Concern was expressed over Mert's condition. No one quite pointed the finger at me. If anyone did I was prepared to explain the rules of baseball and how if a catcher blocked the plate the runner was perfectly entitled to bowl him over even though the rules of softball did differ, involving some despicable line drawn behind home and an illogical force-out on all plays at the plate.

Solange gave Mert an Oxycontin. Maybe not a great idea, moments after a serious concussion, but since Mert was my rival I said nothing.

Scapino was dumped out of his wheelchair so that Mert could be placed in it and wheeled to Scapino's hospice cabin.

Monica wanted to take a shower. Once she left I made eye contact with Brianne = 'To your cabin and step on it.'

"You played really good in the game," Brianne said, removing her duds.

I was about to say "So did you," before remembering she'd dropped several fly balls that had led to at least a dozen runs.

"Should we light incense?" she asked.

"If you want, but I only have a few minutes before Monica gets out of the shower."

"You should tell her maybe."

"We'll see what happens."

"This is only my third time. I don't want to count the first two because they were with Burt and Larry."

"What true horror."

"Larry was polite about it. He only did it to fulfill Leena's wishes, just like if she'd asked him to paint the barn. But it was gross when he got into it."

"You and me should escape this place," I said, not really meaning it, but feeling a little like Marty Sheen in *Badlands*.

"You're sweet," she said.

"How was Burt?"

"Worse, tried to be all sexy."

"Fucking Burt," I said, "Mert never propositioned you?"

"He offered right after Leena's declaration. Too eager, so I turned him down."

"Mert will never know what he missed out on. Mert really blew it. He's probably been blowing it his whole life."

I initiated groping. Unfortunately the shot-clock phe-

nomenon caused flaccidity and my attempt was like the attempt of a workhorse pitcher who gives up seven runs over six innings but his team eventually rallies for the win.

"Sorry about that," I said, after finally getting the win for my stats.

"No worries. It was better than Burt."

"But not better than Larry?" I asked.

"Similar to Larry. Do you know what that Alatragus guy is up to later?" asked Brianne.

"Alatragus and I discussed things and it's been agreed that I have like an exclusive thing with you."

"Oh, that's flattering I guess."

"Well, see you at dinner baby."

57

At dinner Monica sniffed at me.

"So, how are things?" I asked Alatragus. This was a long-running joke in our broad circle, sometimes executed using the variant of "Things, how are they?"

"Not bad, not bad," he said, finishing the joke, the joke being that conversation was usually inane in L-S-C or perhaps allover.

Dinner was linguine in clam sauce, striking me and Monica as strange. But Bella had an industrial-sized can of clams that had to be consumed in some fashion, and surprisingly the sauce was delicious.

With nothing scheduled for after dinner the company splintered into little groups. The game of *Magic: The*

Gathering resumed. A group of girls played the board game *Clue,* who at some point stopped following the rules and so the game turned into chaos with everyone having like four to eight hotels on all their properties before the inevitable bankruptcies caused an early end to the game.

"Wrestling?" Pino asked me, grinning his politician's grin.

Pino and I had loved wrestling in elementary school, and had staged big bouts at recess, suplexing one another and executing pile-drivers, the most dangerous maneuver, banned in many promotions. Somehow no necks were broken and it had always been good clean fun.

During the Attitude era of Stone Cold Steve Austin we'd gathered for big pizza parties with Dan Good, Archambeault, and others. Lac-Sainte-Catherine had the most pizza places per capita of any city in Canada, so truly great za could be had for next to nothing, if that's of any interest to readers of this narrative.

Once the pizza parties dried up I continued to watch WWE until the Anger era and the Monday Night Raw blading massacre perpetrated by Big E Langston. I wasn't entertained or even interested by wrestling in those years, but I was trying to use wrestling as a portal in time. Through the bright coloured ostentation, the familiar moves and story arcs, I sought the pleasure of being young.

With Jenny and Monica in toe, Pino and I hauled mattresses from empty cabins to the interior barn stage. It started with silliness: atomic drops, fireman's carries, airplane spins, but it turned out an ex-boyfriend of Jenny's had been a wrestler on the independent circuit, had taught her his moves, and she regularly tweeted and was retweeted by various indie wrestlers. She was solid in the squared circle and took a fierce-looking bump. She only weighed about 110 pounds and skinny people take way more sympathetic bumps, it's well known.

Alatragus and I constructed an angle in which Alatragus and Monica were the long-standing Macho Man and Elizabeth type duo, and I Lloyd the dastardly heel, with Jenny as my whorish Sensational Queen Sherry-type valet. Timothy dropped in to see what we were up to and we enlisted him as special guest referee.

We worked out a sequence of moves and a finish in which Timothy would take a heel turn on Alatragus and kick him in the face. With Alatragus supposedly concussed I would force a kiss upon Monica (kayfabe love of Alatragus), and Alatragus recovers to hit me with a chair to the spine. On the second run-through Jenny delivered a beautiful hurricanrada to Monica, and we decided our match was good enough to show the rest of the CTW.

Popcorn was made, Scapino but not Mert wheeled in, and chairs were set up. I told Solange what to say and she announced the match. Lewis Orlovsky was announced as special guest timekeeper, and handed someone's watch, but it fell from his hands because his motor functioning had deteriorated so.

Timothy was introduced as Dangerous Timmy Davis.
Monica was introduced as Elise Ivey.
Jenny Caveat was introduced as The Filthy Little Slut.
Alatragus Pino was introduced as John Steel.
Lloyd MacDonald was introduced as Old Boner Stevenson.
Pino and I locked up in a collar and elbow tie-up. When I hit him with a low-blow he ran to Monica for a tag. In true heel fashion I raised a fist at Monica, forcing Timothy to let Jenny tag in, as per the rules of a mixed tag match. Jenny entered with a beautiful drop-kick leading Monica to take an amateurish bump and then rub at her shoulder.

Larry and Burt shook their heads = 'Haven't there been enough injuries for one day?'

The very flexible Timothy misjudged the force of his kick and jarred Pino's head. Alatragus then took this out on me with a vicious chair shot. After the pinfall, to my chagrin, he hoisted Monica on his shoulders in the fashion that Macho used to hoist Liz. Still supine, I shot him a dirty look, but by then all the girls wanted to participate in the wrestling until it devolved into a pillow fight. As I lay prone, Ashley and Brianne jumped on top of me in what we in L-S-C to our great discredit continued to call a "nigger pile."

"Nigger pile!" Candy yelled, and jumped on the nigger pile. When it became difficult for me to breathe I freaked out and accidentally elbowed Brianne in the chin, mashing her teeth together.

She screamed a bit, leading Burt to take charge and say, "Enough now!"

I'm not sure what they call "nigger piles" in more civilized regions. 'All man piles' perhaps?

58

Despite death on the horizon, despite Dan Good and the Bund, despite doom harbingers such as a dick-free Scapino, I was happy to be alive and experiencing the quality of the night.

Timothy, Jenny and Alatragus joined us in our cabin for a game of dominoes. We laughed and drank Cokes I requisitioned from the walk-in refrigerator. As dawn glowed like the perfect pink of Brianne's crescent lips, everyone had fallen asleep except Jenny and me, so we went out for a walk.

"Do you remember in grade seven when Stacey Burroughs wrote that note about wondering what colour Mr. Carlucci's pubic hair was and then someone found it and put it on Mr. Carlucci's desk and then Mr. Carlucci had to then awkwardly address the issue hahahaha?" Jenny asked.

"Felt most bad for Stace, because she was joking, but then also really bad for Carlucci having to acknowledge the idea of Stace thinking about his pubes," I said.

"Yes!" Jenny shrieked.

"Remember when those huge mounds of ice from our snow fort crashed on Phil Echols' neck and Phil Echols was taken to the hospital and things got real grave for a while when it was feared he was paralyzed?" I asked.

"I remember you and some other kids applied your weight to the top of the snow fort to make it crash on him," Jenny said.

"That's how it went, yes."

"Why was everyone so mean to him?" she asked.

"Better him than me. That was always my approach," I said.

"Do you remember riding bikes up Oak Park?" asked Jenny.

"I do. Do you remember when we went to Science North in grade six, about the time kids started to require deodorant, but many weren't yet wearing deodorant, so it smelled bad?"

"I do. And because of the porcupines there, I thought it was the porcupines that smelled, but really it was the b.o., so now whenever I smell b.o. I think of porcupines," she said.

"Do you remember Ed Chouinard's mom?" I asked.

"Poor Chouinard."

Eddy Chouinard's mom had posed for let's-just-say-*niche* Internet pornography and some peers of ours had found it while consuming Internet pornography in the eighth grade.

"Do you remember how it used to feel on the first spring days of the year? And how St. Mark's Elementary carpets smelled on the first day back at school?"

"Of course I remember those things Lloyd."

"Do you remember how important we all were to each other? Even though we forgot each other since?"

"Yes Lloyd."

"I'm glad you're here Jenny. Otherwise I'd have to remember all these things alone."

"That's nice Lloyd."

By morning's complete light, if I wanted to kiss Jenny, it was not out of lust, but out of the old orange thrill of human understanding. To my credit I did not try.

When we entered my cabin Pino's hand was wedged between Timothy's thighs in a hilarious *Planes, Trains and Automobiles* fashion. I presumed this inadvertent because I did not suspect Pino of sublimated bi-curious desires, not even so far sublimated that they might manifest in sleep.

What I did not like seeing, however, was Pino's arm around Monica's stomach, meaning Pino was essentially spooning Monica, so I clapped my hands and said, "Everyone get back to their cabins!"

It was time for Monica's Battalion duties. Alatragus offered to assist, and I didn't want to concede any alone time to him, so I also had to assist.

Monica, wearing giant yellow rubber gloves, reached down past the surface scum and rooted around in the septic sediment to uproot irreducible solids that had settled. Sadly, septic spray sprayed right into my open mouth. Pino and Monica laughed, so I screamed at them and went to shower, certain I'd come down with something, septic sprays intaken orally being about the best transmission process imaginable for anaerobical bacterial infection.

At breakfast they were still laughing about it, so instead of talking to them I shot smokey glances at Brianne and Ashley, and also some Brando-inspired eye squints. When Brianne and Ashley appeared to lose interest in my smokey glances and perhaps hostile-looking squints, I shot smokey glances but fewer squints at the bleached-blonde Penny, whom I had not yet gotten around to, in terms of the whole procreation process.

59

Leena made a surprise appearance at breakfast, appearing dead drunk. She poured coffee into a glass half full with amber liquid, didn't say a word or exchange a glance with anyone, and left.

"The creative process is a difficult one," Solange said in response to the questioning glances of the company, "Don't think it isn't."

Visibly shaken, Solange then announced that Lee would be leading the group in a movement class. This class's primary focus involved rolling over each other on the dusty barn floor. When Pino rolled in the direction of Monica I rolled in such a way as to block him = 'You want to roll over someone, roll over me pal.'

Solange took me aside.

"Lloyd, we need your help. The process of writing this play has been hard on Leena. She's still in the brainstorming stage, and with the festival only two weeks away, we desperately need to start rehearsals."

"Does she need me to punch up some of her pages?" I asked.

"I don't know what that means," said Solange, "But she isn't up to seeing anyone except me, and only me sometimes. What we need you to do is start writing this fucking play. You're a screenwriter right? So writing a play shouldn't be a stretch for you."

"Plus, there are video installations, so that is filmic," I pointed out.

"You got it. So, as you know, the play is a tribute to Dennis Hopper. We want to bring together Hopper's finest moments on film, the most iconic scenes, and then wrap it all up in an apocalyptic bow."

"I can do that. Huge fan of Mr. Hopper's work," I said, conscious that maybe Hoppy himself was watching this all go down.

She set me up in her cabin with Leena's MacBook. It ran Windows instead of the Mac operating system, something I'd never seen before and considered cool. I nodded at Solange and unbuckled the first button on my button-fly jeans.

"Wait, Lloyd," she said, and then showed me this maneuver of running the tips of my fingers over her skin, barely touching her skin, such that goose bumps emerged on the skin. "Oooooh," she said. Solange was nothing if not a "hypnotist collector," to borrow a phrase from the poet laureate of rock and roll.

I made a mental note to apply this skin near-touch technique during all my appointments to make them less soulless and sex trade-y. Once finished, both working hard to catch our breath, she said, "Can I get anything for you?"

"No, but maybe you could send Brianne in around noon. With a sandwich."

She gave me a not altogether positive look, but then said, "Sure, anything else?"

"Maybe Ashley around 3?"

"Fine."

"One last thing. Keep Pino away from Monica while I'm engaged in the creative process. Maybe send him out to scour the wilderness for exotic burl needed for the production or make something to that effect up."

"Done," said Solange.

"Oh and if Ashley isn't available at 3, Penny would be fine also."

Like most writers I can never get down to work immediately. I checked Facebook, but there was nothing resembling legit statuses anymore. Just piked heads and the crap I have laboriously described in previous sections. I checked Monica's email. No emails from her mom. Her DealGetters deals were now announcing deals on like Celebrity Viscera and Debowling Instruments and other things she wouldn't want deals on.

I tried to download screenplays of seminal films like *Easy Rider, Apocalypse Now, Out of the Blue, Speed, Blue Velvet,* etc., but most were alternate versions, poorly formatted, or otherwise unusable. I typed a note in Windows' WordPad program, "Solange, is it possible for the Bund to raid the L-S-C Public Library and grab me a few official screenplays? The ones I'm finding online are unserviceable."

A powerful opening scene was crucial. I figured there was no better place to start than the beginning of Hopper's career, so I opened with the Chickee Run scene from *A Rebel Without a Cause.*

> *Entire cast stands in a circle. Girls wear poodle skirts and bullet bras* (if we can fashion such) *the men have shoe-polish in their hair or whatever can be done to make them look like juvenile delinquents and not old men. Tim-*

> *othy plays James Dean. Alatragus Pino plays the enemy*
> *of James Dean whom James Dean is racing in the deadly*
> *chickee run.* (I'm thinking we can make fake cars out
> of cardboard or whatever the L-S-C CTW has done
> in the past to make fake cars.)
>
> *Monica, as the Natalie Wood character, starts the race.*
> *They race. Dean's enemy/Alatragus crashes from the edge*
> *of the stage.*

I remembered then that Dennis Hopper was barely used
in the original Chickee Run scene. Plus there was nothing
profound or interesting about this opening. I looked at the
books on Solange's shelf. She had a lot of pop-mystical stuff
like *The Celestine Prophecy* and *The Secret*. But she also had the
deeper books of spiritual inquiry like The Holy Quran and
The King James Bible. Flipping through the bible I found
a passage potent enough to kick off my masterpiece in good
old 2 Timothy 3:1-5.

> **Hopper** (I, Lloyd, will play Hopper, at least young
> Hopper, maybe Larry can play old Hopper, because,
> I'm surprised no one has mentioned, Larry bears a
> strong resemblance to old Dennis Hopper) *takes cen-*
> *tre stage, raises arms in Moses-like* Ten Commandments
> *fashion, speaks:* But know this, that in the last days per-
> ilous times will come: For men will be lovers of them-
> selves, lovers of money, boasters, proud, blasphemers,
> disobedient to parents, unthankful, unholy, unloving,
> unforgiving, slanderers, without self-control, bru-
> tal, despisers of good, traitors, headstrong, haughty,
> lovers of pleasure rather than lovers of God, having a
> form of godliness but denying its power.

A decent morning's work behind me, I watched Hopper clips on YouTube to prepare for the afternoon, fell asleep, and was woken when Brianne made the scene. I applied my new arm-touching technique and she said, "Is it just me or are you getting better at this?"

60

Sandwich consumed, genitals rinsed in bathroom, my afternoon writing session commenced with rooting through Leena's files. In her My Documents folder I found a file called "Hopper's Odyssey," read it, and emailed it to myself for future reference. Here is a sample:

> There is a night. There is a night which Brent Steiner wakes in after writing bad review of my visions. There is a lion. Sometimes on the lion's back is a monkey. Sometimes there is a buggy. Scapino has paid, but not enough. I can pretend to ask a question. It is easy to forget, but Scapino will not forget that he refused me. Crows. Crows descend on audience at conclusion of first act—where to collect crows? Get Solange on crow collection? Stick crow up Scapino's stupid tight butt? Satisfactory philosophical lines I bet. Patty Scapino's looks at me post-proposals as though she knew even if she didn't know and me having to wonder if she knew. Scapino sleeping angelic in passenger seat on road trip to North Bay. Scapino shocked at side of road after his sleeping

pants broached and Scapino shouting, "What???"
Just like that "What???" and this sound has forever
defiled my nightly goodnight fantasies. Maybe his
eyes go next. Cut out Scapino's eyes maybe or have
maybe...Candy do. Scapino always fond of Candy
it seemed. Maybe cut out Candy's eyes as well as
Scapino's eyes. Pile up the eyes or put a kebob stick
through the eyes to make an eye kebob. "Sharp, funny, jubilant"—words used to describe me as a young
woman, and yet when reaching into Scapino's pants
I was by then old and undesirable. Terrible awk-
wardness in the car after. LeRoi touching me when
we were teenagers and Scapino's minor resemblance
to LeRoi. Months of Scapino-related doldrums.
Called 'Lousy drunkard' by husband. Triple murders planned. $400 spent on espionage equipment
placed in Scapino's mother's Camry by Solange.
That time the CTW went horseback riding and
how Scapino looked on his horse. Woman's World
Magazine and the limited satisfaction yielded there-
from when Scapino won't even accept a no-strings-
attached in-Camry handjob offer. A big boom from
the mountain! Falsification of documents. My 29th
birthday gave a handjob on Greyhound bus for dar-
ing thrill of it, perhaps why approached Scapino in
same fashion. 29-year-old birthday Leena's offer accepted. Many scenes to finish. Focus on Hopper and
not Scapino's sleep-rod. Channel Hopper as King
Coopa. Actor playing should say "Man," "Groovy"
and "Dig" a lot. Hoped to retire with Scapino in
San Jose, so much for that. Stupid canucks. Should
return to Lewiston. The sweet breath of Scapino.
Jewels not eyes. Straight back unlike hunched back

of non-man husband. No affection, gratitude or love for all I've done for him. No loyalty. Believes he will be a star with his three-point plan. Drinking coffee very quickly after Scapino refusal just past the Outlaw Valley. Picking and choosing my little kingdom here, for what? For whom. For Scapino.

I called out for another plate of food. Candy heard and brought me some Family's Best dill pickle chips, the most dehydrating chip on the market.

"Candy. Did you ever have a thing with Scapino?" I asked.

"No way," she said.

After a pause I asked, "Impregnation? As per Leena's dictum?"

"I suppose."

Afterwards, I considered warning her of eye kebobs, but feared she'd tell Solange and then my own eyes might be put on the kebob. If things got ugly I could always drop a quick word to Candy before escaping with Monica, Jenny, but probably not Pino, although it might pose an issue prying Jenny from Pino. I considered bringing Candy along too, Candy being way cuter than I'd previously given her credit for.

61

I resumed research for the afternoon writing session. I Wiki'd *Night Tide*, a film I'd seen on late night TV that had always stuck with me. A forgettable little movie, but Hopper burned up the screen. As the Sisyphean rock of writerly

progress began to budge, Monica entered with a plate of macaroni salad and garlic bread.

"Can't you see I'm trying to work?"

"Brianne told me you didn't like your sandwich," she said. I blanched.

"That's nice of you. Has Pino been bothering you much?" I asked.

"He's been assigned to watch over Scapino and Mert. Mert seems to be coming around. He tried to grab my butt."

I challenged her on why she needed to be in the medical cabin with Alatragus in the first place, but she only lifted her cheekbones at me in an indication of hostility.

"Bobo had diarrhea," she said after a moment, "And then he ate the diarrhea before I could stop him. Then he vomited up the diarrhea. I had to clean the whole cabin."

"Poor Bobo," I said, "Maybe too much food from the composter. Let's go back to feeding him the dog food we brought."

She sat on my lap. I kissed her small face. Though it would be my record-setting fourth go-round in five hours, for old times' sake, and as a renewal of our devotion to each other, we engaged in a no-nonsense hj/br combo. A mild whiff of Candy's scent wafted to my nostrils. Monica either missed the waft or chose to let it slide.

"Leena is crazy," I said.

After reading the document Monica laughed and said, "I always knew she had a thing for Scapino."

"Should we escape?" I asked.

"And face the Bund?"

"We should have an escape plan in place at least."

"Can Alatragus and Jenny come?" asked Monica.

"Jenny can come."

"No Pino?"

"Why are you so into Pino all of a sudden?" I asked.

"You brought him into the fold. It'd be wrong to leave him to die."

"If we're taking Pino, where do we draw the line? Why not Candy? Why not Ashley, Lee, Larry?"

"Because those people are here of their own volition," said Monica.

I tried to imitate her hostile cheekbone raise, overdid it, and then felt mean and ugly.

Before she could storm off I took her in my arms = 'Look, there may be some funny business with Brianne, Ashley, Solange, Candy, eventually Penny, and so on, but know that you are my number one gal.'

"I don't even like Alatragus," she said softly, "I just wanted to make you jealous."

"Make me jealous with Alatragus and Alatragus pays with his life," I said in a noirish fashion that was 1/8th noir-satire and 7/8th homicidal honesty.

"Just cause you killed a bunch of people doesn't mean you can go threatening to kill non-Angries, Lloyd."

"What else did you do today?" I asked to change the subject.

"Those girls taught me to play *Magic: The Gathering*."

"Don't play that."

"Why not?"

"First it's *Magic: The Gathering,* then it's all-night role-playing weirdness, then cosplay, and then not combing your hair, and where does it end?"

"Talk to Pino and Pino dies, don't play Magic cards, don't stop combing my hair. I hate you for being so bossy," said Monica.

There was a silent thirty-second entropic burn-off of our hatreds.

I told her I'd written her into my opening Chickee Run scene, and would be happy to feature her in others, but she

rightly suspected this might make Solange jealous and cause Solange to kill her.

When Ashley appeared at the door for my 3 o'clock I played it dumb, "Ashley! What a pleasant surprise, what brings you here?" and then made eye signals = 'Make up a lie!'

She said, "Just came by to see what time dinner is at," which was probably the stupidest lie she could have come up with.

"Lloyd needs to work," Monica said, and left with Ashley in tow, a relief because I was not physically or spiritually prepared for go-round #5.

62

My YouTube viewing of the Rudyard Kipling poem *If*, performed by Dennis Hopper on *The Johnny Cash* show, was interrupted by Monica.

"What is it now?"

"Another Bund delivery," she said.

The Bund's Fords were filled with faceless, bloody-crotched bodies.

"Got your bodies here," said the uglier of the two male Bundsmen, whose nametag read Randy.

No one had anticipated a delivery of bodies, so I took charge and said, "Thanks Randy."

Randy produced an invoice. The invoice requested $0 payment in exchange for the 15.00 bodies. Solange signed the invoice.

The short-haired, androgynous girl was again with them. I said to her, "Hey, sorry to bother you, quick ques-

tion—were you with those engineers back in the Bell Drive area?"

Everyone looked at me, considering my query a real face-risking proposition.

"Yes," she said.

"When did you join the Bund?"

"We were always Bund-affiliated. Mr. Good sent us to monitor you."

This brought me the temporary joy of thinking that Dan Good might care.

Randy grunted. The F150 engines ignited while we the L-S-C Community Theatre Workshop dealt with a redolent heap of faceless bods. The flies that flew to the bod-heap ate flesh. The condition of the bod-heap's butts and genitals, due to certain limits of propriety to which I subscribe, will not be described.

"What should we do with these bodies?" asked Solange.

"One option," Monica piped in, "is the walk-in freezer, so that they don't stink up the place."

"I don't want my food in with corpses," said Ashley.

I whispered instructions to Solange. Burt, Larry and Pino were then tasked with wheeling the newly-delivered bods into the barn using the Temagami Music Camp's lone wheelbarrow. No more Lee-taught movement classes in the barn. Just a big bod-stack.

Jenny started crying. Solange recognized this as bad for morale, and sent her on septic check. Monica, under the guise of Battalion experience, followed and comforted Jenny, no doubt accruing resentment from Solange.

When the crowd dispersed, too stunned for *Magic: The Gathering* or other diversions, Solange addressed me, "Lloyd, you have insight into the creative process. Any idea what Leena wants these corpses for?"

"Has to be for *Apocalypse Now*," I said, "You know—the horror, the horror."

"No, what horror?"

"Seminal line from both the text and film," I said, "spoken by Kurtz."

"This is why you're integral to the success of this festival," Solange said worriedly.

Bella, who had not been privy to the corpse dump/Bund visit, emerged from the kitchen and announced dinner. Dinner was Hamburger Helper, very greasy, and aesthetically way too similar to the skinless faces of the barn-stored bods.

Timothy was not at his usual seat. After Burt questioned this, Solange's attention was brought to the matter. When a cabin search came up empty it became clear that Timothy had made a break for it.

63

Solange broke a metre stick over her leg. "Why does everything have to be so difficult?" she asked, and then had a minor actress-y breakdown, wept and writhed on a couch, was comforted by some of the girls, regained her composure, and finally said with the weariness of an overworked stage manager, "Let's hunt him down. Based on our tutorials at the range the other day, we want Candy and Larry riding shotgun. Burt, Brianne, Lee, and Penny can ride in the truck beds. I'll drive the new truck. Lloyd, you're becoming my right-hand man around here, why don't you drive the other one?"

"Can I sit in the middle with Lloyd?" Monica asked.

"I don't care," Solange said. "We can only stick to the main roads and hope Timothy isn't too deep into the wilderness. Doubtful because remember he was always freaking out about blackflies? Lloyd you head east. We'll go west."

The old truck had a standard transmission. I had only driven standard one time previous to the recent motorcycle debacle. Better believe that Burt, from the truck's bed, issued some dirty looks when the truck lurched and jerked. Unfortunately for Burt, Solange had already peeled out of the driveway in the F150, so her directives couldn't be overridden.

Candy sat shotgun while Burt and Lee balanced long-barreled rifles over the truck bed's left and right edges. After a few moments it began to seem like a nice drive. Candy told a story about a part Timothy had played, prompting a sadness = 'Are we really going to kill Timothy?' I had no such intention, but felt I couldn't stray from our designated route or I'd be exposed as an insurrectionist.

"There he is," Candy said, and pointed into the woods, where I could not actually see Timothy, but only the bright red bandanna he wore on his head, indicative of Timothy's low odds out there, lacking the sense to remove a bright red target from his head.

"Burt and Lee must not have seen him," Monica said = 'He doesn't have to die.'

"Candy," I said, "I know you loved Scapino. I know you don't want to kill Timothy."

"I don't," she said.

"We won't tell," Monica said.

I sped up a little. Candy did not shoot. Candy began crying.

"What's wrong?" Monica asked.

"She gave us everything," Candy said.

"I know," said Monica.

Burt was leaning way over the edge of the truck bed, so in the interest of hilarity I took a 90 degree turn as hard as possible into a farm driveway, sending Burt to the gravel road where coincidentally he also separated his shoulder. Afterwards he threatened to shoot me, but by the time he reached his gun he'd been talked out of it by Lee.

Back at the Music Camp, Burt was thrown in the medical cabin with Scapino and Mert. With only two beds, the catatonic Scapino had to be placed on the concrete floor.

Solange returned and asked, "Any sign of him?"

I responded with a confident "No ma'am." But Candy lowered her head, which Solange noticed.

Solange then looked at Lee. Lee said, "We see him, no."

"Where's Burt?" asked Solange.

"Separated shoulder," I said.

"I said Burt not Mert!" shouted Adel.

"Burt's shoulder was also separated," offered Candy.

"That's weird," Solange said. "Well, we can't be hunting Timothy through the woods. We are artists, not mercenaries. He'll be left to the Bund."

"Should we text the Bund or something?" asked Larry.

"Only Leena knows how to contact them," said Solange.

Wanting to show I was in step with the CTW's objectives, I said, "Darn, should have asked the Bund for some official screenplays that could be useful to my process when we had the chance."

No one responded to that, but the vibe = 'When is someone going to challenge this dink?'

Monica and I went to bed early and held each other. We did not whisper of escape because we'd seen how it went for Timothy.

Pino, who'd always been a go-along-to-get-along sort, knocked on our cabin door to ask if we wanted to play dominoes again.

"No, Alatragus, I don't want to play dominoes. I spent the whole day sweating blood to write pages for this production that I'm now in charge of, then dealing with the Bund when the Bund delivered a bunch of unexpected bodies, then hunting down my best male friend in this encampment, so no I don't want to play dominoes."

After he left, Monica said, "He was the one who had to cart away the bodies you know."

That left a bad taste in my mouth, so after Monica fell asleep I snuck out of bed, this time keeping Bobo silent with stern eye contact, headed over to Penny's cabin, knocked, and asked, "Penny, how are things?"

64

In the morning Alatragus was knocking at the door again, wondering if Monica needed help with Battalion duties.

"Get the hell out of here," I hollered, not having gotten much sleep due to the multiple hours it took me to consummate things with Penny.

Breakfast consisted of those last-resort white sausages, causing me to mourn Gary and mom momentarily, but I had to keep those thoughts at bay because there was no sense spending final moments on earth mourning, was my philosophy.

The white sausages resembled the viscera and various innards that had been extruded from the butts of the corpses so I ate only two, Monica one, many of the girls none at all. Larry couldn't get enough down, and kept taking the uneaten sausages.

We did Tai Chi, but our hearts weren't in it. Most people were thinking of the corpse pile, Timothy being hunted by the Bund, the separated shoulders of Mert and Burt, or their own personal losses.

After the session, Solange said, "Now for the unpleasant part of the day. Lloyd tells me these corpses were delivered for a reason. Do not think we're as bad as the Bund or ourselves Angry just because we're now dealing with corpses. It's no different than the dreamcoat in *Joseph* or any other theatrical property this company has used in the past. Leena's vision is going to save mankind. And that vision, according to Lloyd, is so grand and beautiful that it means the heads of these corpses have to be sliced off and put on pikes, and that job isn't going to perform itself."

"I nominate Larry," I said.

"I nominate Lloyd," said Larry indignantly.

"This is something so unpleasant that we should all have a stake in it," said Solange, presumably not intentionally punning with the word *stake*.

Larry found a big pile of fence posts that could be used for head pikes. In the kitchen we commandeered Bella's sharpest knives, but not before an ugly confrontation in which she claimed to need them for cutlets, clumsily tried to hide them, then got in an incredibly dangerous sort of tug-of-war with Lee over one of the knives.

With the two knives we took turns sawing off heads. One has to saw for some time to remove a head, even the head of a half-rotted corpse. All those sinews and tendons were a bastard to cut through. Some of the girls cried. It reminded me of one time when Gary had bought a frozen chicken at a discount grocery store, and when we took it out of the freezer the head was still on. Gary had sawed at the frozen head for a few minutes before eventually saying, "Fuck this," throwing it in the garbage, and ordering Chinese food.

"Why are we doing this?" cried Candy, "Couldn't Leena have asked the Bund to deliver the bodies with the heads already cut off?"

As if summoned from ether, Leena to the soundtrack of the still-playing overture, stumbled onto the scene.

"Who said cut the fucking heads off?" she slurred.

"Lloyd did," said Solange.

"Who in shit is this Floyd character?" inquired Leena.

I smiled, trying to look like a young man open-minded towards handjob offers from 60-year-old theatrical Grand Dame-types, and said, "Pleasure to meet you. Huge fan of your work"

"Who in fuck gonna play Hooper?" Leena demanded, nearly fell, and then turned fiercely at Solange, "Who this Lloyd anyway?"

"A friend of Monica's and a screenwriter," said Solange.

"Perhaps Larry could play older Dennis Hopper. There's an uncanny resemblance," I said, trying to get the focus off me.

"Hey, thanks Lloyd, that's a nice compliment," said Larry.

"Everybody shut up!" yelled Leena, "and put those heads back on those bodies."

She then poured herself coffee, screamed at Bella for some reason, and returned to her cabin.

Penny produced a sewing kit and we laboriously tried to sew a head back on a body, but it took forever and the head kept flopping off, so we decided Leena was too drunk to know the exact number of bods anyway, and we could dispose of the headless corpses easily enough.

We made a big bonfire far from Leena's cabin and burned the bods. It smelled like good barbecue. At lunchtime nobody wanted the cutlets Bella had made with her third-best knife. A shame because those cutlets were the most toothsome entrée offered since my arrival.

65

After lunch Solange invited me to her cabin. I presumed she was interested in randiness, arm-brushing, etc., and to be frank, I was so sickened by head-sewing and other recent atrocities that I had half a mind to decline. But she wanted something else.

"Do you think Leena is crazy?" she asked.

"Yes," I said, a calculated risk, "It's obvious she's crazy. Documents on her computer prove it. Plus she's really heart-broken by Scapino's rejection of her handjob offer."

"For a while I chalked up her decline to artistic temperament, or stress at having to save the world through dramaturgy," said Solange, "but I believe in the Hopper play's importance because I've had the Hopper dreams."

"I too have had Hopper dreams," I said.

"Are we all crazy?" she asked.

"Depends. Members of the CTW may be suffering from a *folie a culte* because Leena is a dominant figure in your lives, and now that she's crazy you're following her just like people followed Murray Applewhite or David Koresh."

Almost to rebuke my statements and prove that we were all crazy, or that Solange and I were at least suffering from a *folie a deux*, an apparition appeared. Do not picture some wispy or translucent wraith. This was a flesh and blood being. I call it an apparition because it appeared out of nowhere and had the precise appearance of a person known dead. The apparition appeared in the form of beloved character actor Scatman Crothers.

"Scatman Crothers!" I said.

"Hello there folks. How are you this afternoon?" he said in his warm-bath tenor voice.

"What and why?" asked Solange.

"Now, there's no cause for alarm ma'am. I've been sent here by the boss to give you all a message, and it concerns what you was just talking about see."

"Loved your work in *One Flew Over the Cuckoo's Nest*," I said, resisting the temptation to cite his best known role as chef Dick Halloran in *The Shining.*

"Why thank you sir!" the apparition of Scatman Crothers beamed, "What I come for is to tell you your thinking is on the money. Hopper's Odyssey must go forward. But Miss Leena can't be at the helm. She gone nuts and too much drinkin'. You'll have to assassinate her. And folks, I know times are tough. I know it's hard to believe what's in front of your own eyes these times. So what I'll do is give you what's called a prophetic vision. The prophetic vision is this: tomorrow or the next day the soundtrack switches from the Overture to Lux Aeterna, which you'll maybe recognize from the same motion picture soundtrack."

Solange fashioned her lips into a pout of consideration until the apparition of Scatman Crothers ceased to be visible.

"Lates Scatman," I said, taken aback at having met such a beloved representative of film history.

"So, listen, are we assassins? Are we in this together?" Solange asked, putting on her motivational cap, the only role outside of pure Artist she was comfortable in.

We exchanged an awkward high-five.

"Leena could be dangerous. She must be sent out of the game in the interest of The Odyssey," I said.

"Tricky thing will be convincing the rest of the company. They worship Leena. You see that. She has done so much for all of us. She has made me what I am. The company will need some new figure to worship," said Solange, "You're the writer now. It'll be your vision. Before we kill Leena we must convince them to worship you."

"Might be hard to convince Burt and Mert, but I'm cool with that," I said, and stroked her arm.

"Now that Leena has been deemed crazy by Scatman Crothers I'm not sure I need to be pregnant anymore," Solange said

"Didn't that dictum come when Leena was believed sane and still channeling relevant details about our journey together?" I asked.

"Nope, that declaration signaled the beginning of the end."

"Gee. Might I ask you not to tell the other girls?"

"How do we convince them of your worth as leader if you continue to take advantage of Leena's crazed orders just so you can do it with a lot of girls?"

"Man. Can you at least leave me Brianne and Ashley?" I asked, sounding a bit desperate.

"So, the dubious orders somehow apply only to them?"

"Maybe the orders aren't required. I think those two are legitimately into me."

"Get a clue Lloyd."

66

I found Monica in our cabin attending to Bobo, who'd been whining all day.

"Poor Bobo," I said, and scratched his head. I mentioned the apparition of Scatman Crothers, and then described him as "the black guy from *The Shining*" for Monica's benefit.

"The main guy?" she asked.

"No, obviously not. That was Jack Nicholson, who is not black."

"But, like, almost the main guy."

"Actor from *The Shining* is all you need to know here. Scatman appears and says we need to kill Leena or else Hopper's Odyssey won't save mankind."

Monica stuck her tongue out of the corner of her mouth in an adorable dumbshow of concentration, and then said, "You shouldn't kill her yourself. Get someone else to do it. Other than me."

"Larry would be perfect. Or Burt or Mert. But they're lost causes since I separated their shoulders," I said. "But right now I've got two things on my plate: producing pages of Hopper's Odyssey and politicking amongst the company to ease my eventual transition into power and maybe find a murder accomplice."

I left the cabin and found Lee in the dining hall.

"What you reading there?" I asked her.

"Spider's Lair."

"Science fiction?"

"The near-future dystopia written in 1982."

"Any accurate predictions?"

"No sir, and they never get the inflation right. Here's this character you know, The Spinner, he order a beer, and it cost him $4.50, and this author make big show to say 'a beer cost whole $4.50 in bar by 2017,' and cue theremin, but beers they cost almost $9 after the tax now."

"Good observation. Well, it's been nice talking to you Lee."

I shot Larry the thumb and forefinger gun and said, "Larry, my man, looking good as always."

I patted Lewis Orlovsky on his skull and wiped some drool from his mouth with my shirt sleeve. He screamed in a way that did not seem altogether hostile.

Bella may not have pulled any weight in terms of power dynamics, but I said to her, "Have to tell you Bella, those cutlets were out of this world."

Then I headed to Brianne's cabin, and lucky for me, Ashley was there also.

"Girls, hey, I realize most times I've dropped by it's been for, well, practical purposes as per Leena's orders, which I was willing to fulfill due to my extreme respect for Leena. But I want to say that while I've appreciated our experiences, I also think you are dynamite human beings worthy of love, respect and the whole spectrum of human emotions. You both mean so much more to me than the three or four times we did it."

"Thanks Lloyd, that makes you way less creepy," said Ashley.

"You thought I was creepy?"

"Not really, but now we definitely don't," said Brianne.

Satisfied in my efforts, I felt the production of pages could wait until after dinner. I went and told Monica of my effective networking.

"That's great," she said, "Also, Jenny stopped by, and I told her what's going on, so she'll help encourage your ascension to leader too."

"You idiot," I said, "She's going to tell Pino."

"What's wrong with that?"

"You don't understand Pino. If he knows there's a power vacuum he's biologically required to seize that power. You should have seen his valedictory aspirations. He's a good guy, but he's got a dark heart for power."

Some spastic coughing from Bobo preceded several minutes of Bobo vomiting up a greenish slime.

67

During a game of catch the next day, Pino proposed that he could act as official leader or executive director while I remained the spiritual and artistic leader. Since spiritual

leadership is always set aside for the biggest flake, I said, "You've had your leadership experiences. Give it up with the leadership in these our final days on earth will ya?"

"You don't understand the crushing demands of running an organization this size. You just want to do it for the girls," Alatragus said.

"The impregnation mandate is over. I'm back to being a one-woman man."

"What? Aww man. I never had a chance to take advantage of the impregnation order."

"Not even once?"

"Well, once, with Lee. You know I've never been that confident around women, so I started with an older woman."

"How'd that go?"

"Good," said Alatragus.

"Alatragus, did you know that Lee is a post-operative transsexual?"

"What does that mean exactly?"

"It means Lee used to be a man, went through a whole physical and psychological process like Bruce Jenner, but then took it one step further by having a surgery, and is now a woman. Only reliable signifier left is the Adam's apple, which you failed to notice, I'll assume. It's nothing to be ashamed of. It's 2016 Alatragus."

As Alatragus scratched repeatedly at his eyelid, I pointed out that we did have some common ground for the time being, in that there'd be no leadership vacuum until Leena was killed.

"So we kill her," Alatragus said.

"It can't be known that we plotted her death, cause then we're tortured and killed by Larry and company."

"That's easy. We suffocate her in her sleep. Make it look like a heart attack or booze-related seizure."

"Pino, you've always been an idea man. That's why as leader I'll be happy to make you my right-hand man."

"Lloyd, when I'm leader I'm sure there will be a position available for you as well. We do go back a ways."

"Agreed, and if you fuck me I'll Tweet about the whole Lee thing, even though as a progressive I don't have a problem with it personally."

68

There was a glinty, Night of the Long Knives-feel at dinner. Pino sat beside me. We weren't scheming or anything, but I wished he'd had the sense to sit somewhere else. Bella set a special piece of lasagna aside for me, with extra parmesan and a basil sprig that no one else got. Monica asked if she could have some, since hers was hard and shriveled, but I said no.

Larry came by and said, "Some weather we're having isn't it?" proving my long-running theory that guys like Larry would be chatting about the weather during any and all levels of atrocity. Lee came by and touched Pino's neck, causing Pino's face to turn red.

"Good evening, Lee," I said, seizing an opportunity to campaign with Lee while Pino freaked out over L-S-C-ingrained gender norms.

I took Solange aside, and told her about our plan, also taking credit for the plan. I touched her arm in a conciliatory way = 'I know Leena meant much to you and soon she'll be out of the game," but Solange mistook it for a light arm brush and said, "Really Lloyd, still? You know, I hate you so much. I'm going to say a few last words to Leena."

Alatragus, Jenny, Monica and I sat in our cabin drinking coffee amidst crackling pre-murder tension. I found coffee neurotoxic and didn't drink it often because it made me jittery, so as my legs jostled everyone looked at me = 'Can this guy pull off a smooth, undetectable murder?' Discussion ensued that maybe Jenny should commit the murder because she was graceful and could sneak into Leena's cabin in silence. But it was deemed she might lack the strength and murderous spirit to hold the pillow over Leena's face.

At 4 am Pino and I crept towards Leena's two-story cabin. We opened the door as slow as possible, but of course being like an ancient redwood barn door it creaked like crazy. We'd anticipated Leena would be passed out, but drunks have their lucid moments, and she was sitting at a desk, alert, with a water glass full of bourbon.

An awkward moment passed. Pino and I looked at each other = 'Too late to just bail?' Then Pino, needing a leadership vacuum, ran up, overturned Leena's chair, held down her shoulders and ordered me to find a pillow.

I didn't know where her pillows might be, and realized we should have brought our own murder pillow. As I scrambled to find one, Leena overtook Alatragus and was drilling him with old lady slap punches.

I knocked the wind out of her with a kick to the stomach, which I'm not proud of as, again, a feminist who abhors violence against women. The only thing left to do was hold her down and suffocate her with a dusty old rug. Once she stopped breathing the apparition of Scatman Crothers appeared and said, "Some fine asphyxiatin' boys."

"Who is that?" Pino asked.

"Apparition of Scatman Crothers," I said, "Did Jenny not mention him?"

"And now ghosts," said Alatragus.

We debated a "Goodbye cruel world"-type note, remembered the death was supposed to be natural, and crept back to our cabin where Monica and Jenny waited for an update.

"She broke my damn nose," Pino said in that whiny tone of the broken-nosed.

"I've seen the nose snapped back into place in movies, want to try that?" I asked.

No one thought this was a good idea, but Pino yelled, "Do it!" to prove he was a man after being overpowered by a 65-year-old woman. I tried and failed. Alatragus shrieked. I apologized, mostly for Jenny's benefit.

Then the problem of explaining the broken nose dawned on us.

"Only one option," said Monica, "Lloyd caught Pino sleeping with me and broke his nose as revenge."

Pino nodded. We all nodded.

I couldn't sleep because of the coffee. Instead I ruminated on the escalating number of murders I'd perpetrated, petted Bobo, and engaged in a long overdue hj/br combo that I had to wake Monica up for.

69

Pino didn't arrive immediately at breakfast and I feared his absence would cast suspicion on us. Breakfast was again terrible white sausages. When Bella offered me two extra I declined, citing a need to watch my figure even though I weighed only 148 pounds. Pino finally emerged and skulked to a seat not beside me but nearby.

"OMG what happen?" asked Lee in her heavy accent, actually saying the letters OMG.

"Nothing serious," Pino replied, "Little run-in with Lloyd. We've sorted it out though."

"I bust him!" Lee said, raising a fist.

"No, no, I had it coming," Pino said, an old political hand sliding into his talking points.

"Coming, no! What could you have done?"

"Fooled around with Lloyd's woman."

At this Lee raised her fist in the direction of Monica. It dawned on me that because Lee lacked reproductive capabilities she wouldn't have presumed Pino's sexual exchange with her was related to Leena's impregnation orders. She evidently considered Pino her man.

Monica did one of those sucking-lips-back-from-teeth gestures = 'My bad' and 'I'm an idiot, sorry,' at the same time. Lee got in her face, waved an index finger, but fortunately did not strike Monica because Lee had wirey arms and had probably thrown a few punches in her time. Lee then sat beside Pino and stroked his hair, which Pino discouraged, no doubt considering the unfavourable attitudes of three conservative old men towards Cisgendered-man-on-trans-woman intercourse.

Solange took me aside and I told her the job was done. Afterwards I performed Tai Chi with zeal to show I was an integral part of the company who wouldn't be asking any hard questions about the measurable merits of Tai Chi on an acting company. When Lewis Orlovsky was in the downward dog position I hilariously pretended to penetrate Lewis from behind, and everyone had a good laugh about that, especially Larry, who loved that type of humour. I caught Pino checking out Monica's downward dog. That really irked me because there were Brianne, Ashley and several others he could have been checking out.

After concluding the Tai-Chi, Solange excused herself and walked up to Leena's cabin. I kicked at bodies in the corpse-pile. Some in the company considered this morbid, so I said, "Might as well get familiar with the properties to be used in this production now."

Solange ran down from Leena's cabin and came straight for Ashley and Brianne, the senior ranking girls. The three of them went to the cabin and returned sobbing. Solange was wise to rely on their legit tears rather than try to sell the performance by herself. I'd seen Solange in a couple CTW plays, and despite all her capital A-Actressyness, she was not a good actress.

"She's dead!" they sobbed.

"Alcohol," Larry said introspectively, "Got my dad too."

Lee reached for Pino's hand to comfort him, but he pulled it away and itched in the direction of his broken nose. Monica was sent to the medical cabin as bearer of bad news. All those therein were doped up on Oxy so the news didn't much register.

"What now?" asked Penny.

"Plan a memorial I suppose," I said, stepping into the leadership void.

"I can produce," Pino said, "I knew her the least, so I'll remain detached and professional in the memorial's production."

"Fine," said Solange, "But we have to move forward with the play. That's the only reason the Bund is keeping us alive. Plus it may save mankind."

"Not without Leena's vision," Brianne cried.

"It will have to be Lloyd's vision now. He's had access to her notes. He's a screenwriter. We must trust his vision," said Solange.

"Let's put it to a vote. I think it should be my vision, maybe, cause I'm the oldest," said Larry.

"Larry," I said, "No offense, but no way this is going to be your vision. But I'm definitely casting you as the older Hopper whenever the older Hopper is called for."

Larry bounced his head around = 'I can live with that.' It was doubtful he expected it to be his vision, and was only bartering to secure a meaty role.

"She wanted to be cremated," Solange said, "We'll burn her tonight after the memorial. The whole cast is at your disposal Alatragus. You'll want to employ anecdotes, songs, interpretive dance, maybe some archery since we spent so long learning archery and won't likely use it in the play."

I didn't like Alatragus getting all that leadership time in with the company, but I had to write pages or I wouldn't have a leadership leg to stand on myself. I asked Monica to come with me to the writing cabin. At first she was flattered to be involved in the creative process, but then visibly soured when I said, "Listen Monica, due to murdering Leena and all the coffee last night I barely got any sleep. Do you think you could bang out a few pages while I grab a quick nap here in this cabin?"

"Lloyd, I'm not a writer."

"What writer? Find Dennis Hopper quotes online, weave them into a scene, and I'll revise when I wake up."

A great rush of air was exhaled from her, so I threw her a bone. "I'm going to get some chips. Do you want anything?"

"Maybe a pop," she said, which is what Canadians call soda.

As I was getting the chips and pop I noticed Bella preparing an industrial-sized bowl of tuna salad.

"What's all the commotion?" she asked.

I hated to break it to her. "Leena died," I said.

Bella broke down sobbing, put her head on my shoulder, and I was trapped comforting her for at least 2-3 minutes until finally I said, "I understand what you're going through," and gingerly lifted her head off my shoulder so that I could walk away.

70

Through the kitchen's back window I saw stretching exercises led by Solange. This heartened me because it meant Pino wasn't seizing the opportunity to lead as presented. Appropriate memorial preparation would have involved brainstorming memories of Leena, practicing shooting arrows into a target, or choreographing dances, which I suppose the stretching could have been in preparation for, except Solange was shouting about purifying the instrument, meaning it was the same bullshit as always.

Back in the writing cabin I took my nap. As in about 40% of dream experiences, I was haunted by nightmares of Dan Good.

The dream consisted of not so much memories as new scenarios sprung from historic tensions between us. In the dream Dan and I are responsible for transcribing calculus notes in a University of Toronto classroom for some reason, and his calculus notes are beautiful, all the delta and epsilon symbols inserted perfectly, subintervals expressed properly, instantaneous centres evoked through very few keystrokes, rotated plates keyed in somehow, whereas I had to write the words "rotating plates." It soon became clear that trying to express a calculus equation linguistically was a fool's game. On my turn, trying to type in an epsilon, which looks like this incidentally, ϵ, I wrote: 3(backwards). Dan is severely let down by my backwards 3 epsilons, and informing his contempt is the troubling sense that I'm still thinking of him frequently. The calculus notes are minimized, exposing a dream diary detailing dreams of our shared youth, which creeps Dan Good out considerably. He can't reconcile this dream-bond with the hockey-watching-normal-Canadi-

an-dude image he strives to project. Instead he criticizes quality of epsilons, quality of endpoint values, quality of tangential directions as typed by me.

"Why do you stick with these bankrupt ideals? Hockey Night as some sweaty-bearded, missing-toothed saviour?" I ask Dan Good.

He throws out a venomous, "Have a nice life" = 'We are done' and I try to tell him to have a nice life with equal venom, but it's known I'd cling in Sal Minneo fashion if allowed.

After describing the dream to Monica I confided, "Dan was constantly rejecting me in all these little ways. For example, he started golfing before me, and was always ashamed of my golf etiquette. Like deeply ashamed. He was cruel, but in this weird, 'I'm trying to save you,' type-way. Maybe because he realized that the way I was would never cut it in L-S-C, and to live and be happy in L-S-C was the real heaven and to come to any other end was to confine one's self to purgatory."

"Wow," said Monica, not contributing much, but at least projecting a bare minimum of empathy.

"I won't lie. I paraphrased some of that from a journal entry of mine," I said.

"Maybe you can find some new friends even though it's end times," suggested Monica.

"I'm afflicted by Dan like the kid who always sought his father's approval and never got it must feel and dream about his father. Dan Good himself has pretty serious father issues incidentally. Like his dad rinsing the driveway with manic focus and castigating Dan if Dan didn't wash the driveway up to his father's standards, and so then Dan taking his driveway standards out on me because that's what people do."

"Strange that Dan would be leader of the Bund eh?" asked Monica.

"He's charismatic. People gravitate towards him. Maybe he's not even Angry, only exploiting the Bund for his own protection. That's the type of thing he'd do."

"What's he like?" asked Monica.

"The more aggressive aspects of my personality are basically me imitating him. Except with him it's all imbued with and buttressed by off-charts levels of boyish charm," I said, and then added, "That's also paraphrased from a journal entry."

"It's neat that you write a journal," said Monica.

"Another possibility I hesitate to even consider or mention, but I always want to be honest with you Monica..."

Her mouth twisted at this because of the recent litany of lies I'd subjected her to.

"What is it?"

"It seems odd that end times are being produced by my favourite director, and that the end times are largely filmic in nature and I love film. Film is a beloved medium I guess. But then for the central figure in my psyche to be the leader of the regionally all-powerful Bund seems too coincidental, like it's all programmed for me."

"Meaning we're not real. That we are programmed," said Monica.

"Are you programmed?" I asked her, and for a terrifying second expected to wake up from a dream.

"No, I'm not programmed. At least not any more than you feel programmed," said Monica.

"Good."

"That's kind of psychotic, thinking no one is real but you, you know?" said Monica.

"It's been bugging me, but now that you confirm you're not programmed I choose to believe you. Unless you're programmed to say you're not programmed, but that's a can of worms regarding issues of free will that neither you nor I are

qualified to discuss in much depth."

"You want to work on this script. I made some notes," she said.

I read over her notes, cherry-picked from a couple You-Tube biographies.

"We should explore the James Dean thing," I said, "Hopper was a minor toady to James Dean, sometimes equal, sometimes toady. I can put my Dan Good issues into that box. It's important this play have something of me in it, for it to have substance."

"But won't Dan Good be weirded out by that and maybe kill us on the spot?" asked Monica.

"All I know is this vision has to be the truest vision I can produce."

"Maybe it should just be really entertaining instead," said Monica.

"See now you're on the right track," said the apparition of Scatman Crothers, then present in cabin.

"Whoa," said Monica.

"Monica—Scatman," I said, "Scatman—Monica."

71

I stepped out for air and to my surprise Lewis Orlovsky stood at the door, not knocking, just standing, swaying more like. This was a surprise because Lewis was considered lacking in any and all personal agency.

Lewis Orlovsky's predicament stemmed from hockey being the entire source of his self-worth. In grade eight he'd

been on the much-vaunted Bantam rep team, largely because of his size, as he was a lumbering, unskilled player. As he got older, and his rep teammates went on to play Triple A and even the nearly-God-like-in-L-S-C Junior A hockey, Lewis fell to lowly Double B. Even in Double B he had a tendency to skate with his head down, hence, like Eric Lindros before him, frequent concussions.

Before concussions mushed his brain, Lewis had been the quintessential modern bully. Not holding kids up by ankles while lunch money sprinkled to the ground, or giving wedgies, as seen on television, but simply being cruel to the weakest person in his vicinity at any given time. I'd been the victim at times, but I was far from the most persecuted, so I can't complain much. What made him the quintessential modern bully was that on other occasions, maybe when it was just you and him, or maybe with a few others around, he'd inquire about your family, your interests, and act like a decent person. It was difficult to reconcile his abusiveness with his genuine desire to know how your great aunt's surgery had gone.

Orlovsky had once flung dog shit at Chouinard at a football game; laboriously scooped shit on a stick and flung it right in Chouinard's face. Another time I saw him giving Chouinard a ride home. He was the type of L-S-C male adolescent who went around flicking testicles with his knuckles. Not only the nuts of the downtrodden either, but also the nuts of his popular peers.

The first symptom of the concussions was aggression. An early warning was when he masturbated into his palm in a hockey dressing room and made a guy who would have ranked at least 72 on a popularity scale of 1 to 100 lick the semen off his hand. In homophobic L-S-C this signified maybe Lewis couldn't be trusted. Then followed long delays

in speech, a tendency to drool, frequent collapses. It got so his peer group no longer found it hilarious when he flicked their testicles.

As his eyes' glaze grew impenetrable, Chouinard and other persecuted parties began exacting revenge, tripping him, slamming Lewis Orlovsky into lockers just as he'd slammed a million torsos into lockers. Sometimes former friends would come to Lewis' defense, but then he'd scream aggressively, or appear disoriented, and high school kids simply don't deal with that type of behavior. Eventually he fell even beneath Chouinard on the popularity scale, which we'd have thought impossible after Chouinard's mom was seen in niche pornography.

Once every persecuted party had gotten their licks in on Lewis it became tasteless to pick on him, but not quite as tasteless as it was to pick on another classmate of ours, Re-tarted Steve; because, developmentally delayed all along, R. Steve had never hurt anybody. So by the end of high school, when some previously aggrieved party slammed Lewis Or-lovsky's already mushy brain into a locker there was a sense of, "Well, maybe you were entitled to that one, but try to take it easy on him going forward."

Though he played hockey for almost as long as he was capable of standing upright, eventually his goal of a hockey career was curtailed by his inability to process spoken language. At this point his mom enrolled him in the CTW. The CTW was something he had actively mocked during his neurologically-intact years, but Orlovsky's mom need-ed a place to drop him off for a few hours so he wouldn't be screaming at her and flicking at her non-extant testicles. The CTW, always sensitive to the differently-abled, had carted him out in a number of roles over the years. After a while he became something of a mascot.

It is testament to the decency of the CTW that in end times they continued to spoon-feed him baby food and make him drink a certain amount of water each day. Often he soiled himself, but no one in the CTW was interested in rectifying this, so due to stink, he was given a wide-berth except when being fed either by Bella, or one of the girls who Bella brow-beat into doing it.

Based on all that, we were surprised to see him at the door. But it made sense when I saw a note pinned to his chest that read, "Lloyd, this memorial is going off the rails. We need a writer down here ASAP. The play will have to wait. – Solange."

Remembering a couple times he'd been a jerk to me, I gave Lewis a swift kick in the ass as he was stumbling back towards Solange. He went pinwheeling down a small hill, fell down, and started crying, causing Monica to chastise me.

72

My contribution to the memorial was a major one, and maybe the brightest feather in my artistic cap up to that point in history, even if the use of the choral refrain did have a strong 'high school assembly' vibe.

I'd interviewed each member of the CTW, with Monica transcribing on Leena's MacBook, then I compiled the best lines into a piece that the members took turns reading.

Chorus: *I miss Leena because:*

She taught me it was okay to strive for great things even though L-S-C isn't known for great things.

Chorus.

She showed me that art was important. And that a person could live for art if they wanted, not just do art to pass the time.

Chorus.

She helped me beat my stuttering problem.

Chorus

She taught me that it wasn't embarrassing to go to the movies alone in the afternoon if you wanted to.

Chorus.

She provided a sanctuary for thoughtful, creative kids in an uncreative town.

Chorus

She showed me acting ain't for sissies as I'd previously thunk.

Chorus.

She gave me a family that was better than my own family because my own family was mean.

Chorus.

She showed me there was more to life than the Central Mall and the stupid people in my grade.

Chorus.

She taught me that my beauty didn't mean as much as I thought it did.

Chorus.

She told to me I want my surgery I should get surgery and not worry about what Henri my brother say.

Chorus.

Gaaaave me plaaace to…(Lewis, whom I included because, theatrically, you can always get a cheap pop with a guy like Lewis struggling against adversity.)

Chorus.

Used to drive me to my job at Subway when my mom got sick.

Chorus.

Was the best actor of us all but never tried to steal the spotlight, and only acted in plays when there was a gaping hole that needed filling.

Chorus.

Also drove my mom to her appointments when my mom got sick.

Chorus.

Provided me with all of my friends, all of you.

Chorus.

Drank about 8 750 ml Diet Dr. Peppers a day.

Chorus.

She showed me you could be old and set in your ways and still do something fun with a lot of young people.

Chorus.

Always smelled fantastic.

Stage direction: The corpse is ceremonially carried and dropped into the fire.

I brought the finished product to Solange who beamed at its quality.

"This is why it's your vision Lloyd," she said.

Alatragus heard this and haughtily ordered Larry to prepare properties. Solange and I worked out the theatrical movements and music that would best accompany my composition. Jenny picked flowers for the memorial, the practicality of which put even her above Pino in the leadership race. I picked up a crab apple and chucked it at Alatragus' head.

"Come on now," said Larry, not one for excessive horseplay.

73

The Memorial was a decent one given the limited resources. Jenny opened by throwing flowers in a fashion perhaps better suited to a wedding. Lee sang a song by Nana Mouskouri. My composition was read by the cast, verses not necessarily spoken by whoever contributed them originally, e.g. Larry speaking the part about surgery encouragement.

We didn't have anything resembling a casket, so Leena's corpse was placed in a plastic sack that had come with an Ikea mattress. The burning plastic left an acrid smell, followed by the now-familiar smell of burning bod.

To everyone's dismay the avenging spirit of Leena rose out of her burning corpse and screamed, "You have cast me into hell!"

"Maybe you aren't in hell," suggested Brianne hopeful-ly, "Maybe you just think you're in hell because your body is burning in the bonfire."

"You fat cow, I've been in hell for the last five million years. Time is different in hell. Ever since that tall skinny bastard killed me I've been rotting and regenerating, having my skin rubbed off by sandpaper only to regrow skin that is sand-papered off again, offering tons of cruelly-declined handjobs, reading and re-reading bad reviews of my plays by Brent Steiner. I could go on."

"Hell's as bad as they say huh?" said Larry, only com-fortable using the tone of small talk.

"Hell is worse than they say Larry, but you'll know that soon enough," said Leena's avenging spirit.

Larry darkened at this, figuring himself a good man not destined for hell.

"Who does she mean by the tall skinny bastard?" asked Ashley.

"I bet it's Scapino!" I said.

"Scaaaaaapinoooooooo," she howled in an immortal hell howl.

"Was it Scapino?" asked Solange.

"Scaaaaaapinooooooo."

"Seems like it was Scapino," I said quickly.

"Must have been Scapino," added Alatragus Pino.

"Cuuuutt his faaaaaaace and eeeeeeat it! Kniiiiiiiiiife his buuuuutt!" howled demon Leena.

"We will. We sure will," said Monica.

She continued to yell Scapino with the many a's and o's as written above until it turned into a high frequency pitch and her spirit apparition exploded into the night air.

"I guess we knife Scapino's butt now," I said in a flat tone.

The procession of knife rapists and face slicers made their way up the hill, borrowed knives from Bella's cutlery

drawer without asking, and entered the medical cabin. Burt and Mert looked mighty alarmed.

"Relax," said Larry, "We didn't done come for you," which I considered an affectation because Larry's speech was usually grammatically-sound.

"Who wants to do it?" Solange asked, with a vicious flick of her neck that drew on her experience playing Lady Macbeth.

"I'll do it," I said, not wanting to knife a butt, but knowing the knifer of Scapino's butt was a shoe-in for CTW leader.

"Let me do it," said Alatragus. We argued until it was compromised that Pino would knife the butt and I would slice the face. But slicing the face ended up being a three man job where Larry had to hold down the squirming Scapino, Pino had to stretch the skin out, and I had to make the incisions and pull away the skin. So really Pino got double leadership points in the whole Scapino bloodbath. Scapino moaned for a while until Candy put him out of his misery by cutting his throat. RIP Scapino.

We realized no one had eaten Scapino's face. Since there were no volunteers the face skin was fed to Bobo, which probably wasn't doing Bobo any favours in terms of his digestive issues.

74

It was agreed that so grisly a happening was hard on the psyche, and we should all retire to our cabins for silent reflection, to decompress. In our cabin Bobo cut into my silent reflection time by coughing up a piece of face flesh. I put a pillow over my head and rationalized, said sorry

to Scapino, but did not think to ask forgiveness from a higher power.

Solange came to the cabin door saying we needed make-work projects to keep the cast's mind off recent events. An insurrection meant the play would not be performed, and as individuals we would fall victim to the Bund. The fact that we ourselves had now perpetrated Bund-like butt-knifings and face-slicings was not broached.

In the spirit of *Apocalypse Now/Heart of Darkness,* Candy, Brianne, Penny and Ashley were assigned to dig a hole in front of the barn stage that we claimed was for the production. Larry, Lee, Leanne, and Lewis dug a hole in the back of the property for reasons equally 'impossible to divine.' At one point Lewis took a bad spill into the hole and Larry had to drag him out, which was hard on Larry because he was old and arthritic and Lewis Orlovsky weighed about 250 pounds.

Solange, Pino and I strategized the way forward over cokes in the kitchen.

"Lloyd, as writer you'll be revered anyway," opened Solange, "so Pino manages day-to-day operations. Meanwhile I'll keep everyone's spirits up and creative juices flowing."

"So I'm like the GM?" asked Pino.

"More like the day-shift manager," I said.

Bella came back in and insisted she had to start her baking, ending the leadership talks in general détente. I fist-bumped with Pino to let him know we were still civilized men, still St. Michael's alumni who would not pull a pearl harbor job on one another.

It was Candy's birthday, so after dinner we celebrated with cupcakes. But Candy was sad over Scapino and burst out crying when presented with her cupcake, causing Solange to throw a bunch of cupcakes across the dining hall in

a rage. Everybody retired off in little cadres to scheme, plot, and cast aspersions.

75

Maybe it was the tension in the air, but it almost seemed like Lux Aeterna, which had indeed started at dawn the day after Scatman's prophecy, grew louder and creepier over the next few days. Once the 'artificial holes' were dug the cast started demanding that rehearsals begin, but I was reticent to hand over the one Chickee Run scene I'd composed.

In the writing cabin, I found it hard to generate ideas. I transcribed scenes from the dubious online screenplays and then employed William Seward Burroughs' cut-up method on them, but this didn't produce anything I'd want to put my name on. Still, pages I could hand over if absolutely necessary.

One day Bella baked oatmeal cookies. On another the entire cast picked wildflowers. On yet another Leena's charred ashes were put in an ornamental hat box with some of the wildflowers. Larry and Lee had an arm wrestling match one evening that was enjoyed by all.

Pino always seemed to be in Solange's ear, which I didn't like one bit, so I tried to get in her ear as well, but I guess as an ex-lover she'd built-up some contempt for me, and I felt that feeling of not being in on something.

One warm afternoon we all went swimming at a small pond about a kilometer from the camp. Some of the girls wore bathing suits and others swam in their underwear. This produced in me a melancholy because I had made love to most of

those girls and knew I'd never make love to them again. We held chicken fights, and Monica and I bested all comers until Lee got on Pino's shoulders and Lee easily sent Monica to the water. I proposed a new round of Chicken Fights with Ashley as my partner, but Ashley declined. Never again would I be in any kind of proximity to Ashley's crotch.

At dinner we all had that post-swimming glow, and it was easy to forget how tragic the circumstances were or that I needed some kind of James Dean-Hoppy-toady theme that I wasn't skilled enough or emotionally erect enough to write.

Once we had retired for bed that evening Jenny came to our cabin.

"Alatragus has been plotting with Solange, and there's going to be a bloody coup against you tonight," she said.

"A coup? I haven't even assumed power," I said.

"Pre-emptive coup I suppose," said Jenny.

"Fuck sakes," said Monica.

"He's told some of the girls that you killed Leena and they believe him. They're going to swarm you tonight. You have to escape before then," said Jenny.

"Do you want to come with us?" I asked her.

"I'll be safer here. No reason for them to turn on me next that I can see," said Jenny.

I'd seen Solange place the Ford F150 keys in a drawer in the kitchen. After Jenny's warning I went and took them. It was weak coup planning not to have hidden those keys from me. I also grabbed some Mr. Noodles and stuffed them into the pockets of my cargo pants. I went to the writing cabin and grabbed Leena's MacBook because I didn't want to lose what little work I'd written.

It dawned on me that I would never write Hopper's Odyssey or save mankind. Solange must have grown sick of my low productivity and figured Larry or someone could write the play.

It was a nervous couple hours anticipating our escape. This wasn't like the unease I'd felt over Leena's madness; this was an actively-plotted coup. There would only be a small window between the standard CTW time of departure for the sleepytown (11:00) and the coup's scheduled midnight attack time.

Monica and I debated whether or not to bring Bobo with us. What if Bobo were to bark? But if we didn't take Bobo could the CTW be trusted to take care of him or would they kill him out of failed coup spite?

As we snuck around the back of the camp, Bobo in tow, I had the perverse feeling that I'd miss the place. Maybe it was the tall grass and the fresh wind, or the fun I'd had playing baseball or wrestling, fun that had been lost to me since high school, more likely it was the girls.

We made it easily to the F150 while Pino's squad planned the coup in some cabin. I turned the engine on and peeled the hell out of there. We hit the open road where we'd try to get past the Bund into some other region where there was no Bund, no Chthonic sightings, no engineers, no marauders marauding. We rolled down the windows and the night air on the highway is always a fine thing.

76

We drove towards Parry Sound, figuring something as batshit weird as the Knife Rapists'/Face Eaters' Bund could only exist in northern Ontario. We only had two 500ml bottles of water, so no way to prepare the Mr. Noodles properly. It's not like we had a pot or a bowl or a heat source anyways, so

we just sprinkled the salt dust over the noodle cluster and crunched it on down.

"Boy, that doesn't taste very good," said Monica.

I felt guilty. If I'd stood down and let Pino assume power then we'd be eating Bella's cutlets, leisurely killing time until our performance for the Bund.

We passed a young woman convulsing on the side of the road. She had a sign reading "Need Water," that evoked our empathy, but we didn't have any extra water so we kept on driving.

"Check out that green mist," Monica said.

"That's the mist that consumed Chicago I bet."

In the distance was a ferris wheel. In the distance was The Zipper. In the distance spun a Gravitron. In the distance we saw another travelling circus. I explained to Monica about the twenty-two consecutive travelling circuses I'd seen on my way to rescue Regan and Emerald.

"Worth a try," she said.

We drove to it and in the parking area there was a teen-age guy in an orange reflective vest directing cars with a wand. Never thought I'd be so happy to delicately back into a parking space, which, along with parallel parks and three-point turns, had never been a specialty of mine.

I approached the reflective teen and asked, "Who's running this thing?"

"That would be Everett Moon," he said.

"Bund affiliated?" I asked.

"I'm not picking up what you're putting down," said the young man.

"Knife Rapists'-Face Eaters'?" I asked.

"Never heard of it," he said.

We walked to the ticket booth and I was surprised to find two twenties in my wallet from the days preceding

the Anger. The same twenties had been in my pocket when Blind Harv was consumed at the call centre. I bought us each a large fountain soda and a chili dog. The large fountain sodas came with free refills that we took advantage of. I have always loved fountain soda.

"I don't know what's happening Lloyd," said Monica, "But I have almost $100 on me. Let's go on some rides."

We argued about whether to go on the Ferris wheel, which was romantic but not all that exciting according to Monica, or the Zipper, which was Monica's type of thrilling ride but something I'd spent a lifetime avoiding. The eventual compromise was the Gravitron, that spinning oval-shaped ride where you stick to the walls by means of extra gravity. After the Gravitron we ate some nachos. We held each other by our respective waists and laughed. Maybe the CTW was just having one bad *folie a culte* trip and we were geniuses for getting out.

We met a little girl covered in *Teen Wolf*-levels of hair. Then we saw Everett Moon. We recognized him as Everett Moon because he wore a nametag that read Everett Moon.

"Greetings," I said.

"Hello," said E. Moon, "What brings you here?'

"Narrowly escaped from a cult-like acting group, expected to be killed by the Bund, Knife Rapists'-Face Eaters' Bund that is. We sure are happy we found this place," I said.

"Sounds like you got out of somebody's bad dream," said the hairy girl.

"I had had that feeling," I said, looking at Monica = 'I was trying to tell you it might be a programmed reality, idiot!'

"This is Chaos' dream," said the girl.

"Who is Chaos?" I asked.

She indicated Everett Moon with her eyes = 'Everett Moon is also Chaos.'

"Chaos is the strongest dreamer in northern Ontario. You'll be safe here," said the hirsute girl.

"That's excellent," Monica said, "Is there anything we can do?"

"Yes," said Chaos. "We need a hypeman for the ring-toss game."

Monica stripped down to her bra because all the other hypemen had scantily-clad babes with them. I called out to the marks, "One throw for a dollar, five for three, get the ring on the stick win a big teddy, everybody wins something, nobody walks away a loser!" and Monica made kissing faces at the men and generally did what a hypeman's loose woman should. Many marks came to pet Bobo and then I reeled them in by disparaging their masculinity.

When the patrons dried up we pulled down the metal grate that covered the ring-toss booth's opening, borrowed some dirty couch pillows from another carny and fell asleep after a quick hj/br combo. When we woke in the morning we were in an abandoned shed and some mice had chewed the plastic wrap off our Mr. Noodles. Chaos had either woken up or moved on. No more travelling circus.

77

Our truck was the only one in a dusty gray lot. There wasn't a hot dog or soda fountain to be seen.

"This sucks," said Monica.

"Want to just cower here for a bit?" I asked.

"Guess so."

We cowered for the entire day, ate our second pack of Mr. Noodles at night, drank the rest of the water, and set out to find more water and food.

"What about Dennis Hopper?" asked Monica.

"I suppose it doesn't matter."

"Skidman Cromwell?"

Lacking the energy to correct her, I said, "Same."

"Seems disappointing that it all led to nothing. That it was a bunch of nonsense," said Monica.

"It's a nonsense world Monica. At least we had a few laughs along the way."

"Is that your mom?"

There on the side of the highway was my mom. My heart leapt at the sight of the woman who'd raised me, brought me McDonalds 4/5 school nights during elementary school despite her hating McDonalds on an ideological level, bought me bathing suits, packed my lunches, set up sprinklers for me to run through, taught me how to teach Pierre tricks, been my primary companion during the years between the Dan Good falling out and the introduction of Monica into my life, introduced me to deodorant when I'd started to smell, rented better movies than the movies my peers were exposed to, quit smoking because of my asthma, always let me win in foot races when I was five through eight or whenever you stop foot racing your mother, quoted Blake as her insanity dawned, took me to my first Sudbury Int'l Film Festival when I was about 14.35, encouraged the better angels of my nature and believed in them even in my scummiest years, turned a blind eye to more than one Kleenex wad over the years, hemmed my jeans though she was not the jean-hemming type, bought me expensive Tommy Hilfiger products when I was certain they were what I needed even though she knew better, always made iced tea incredibly weak because that was how I liked

it, exclaimed enthusiastically at every foul ball in my softball games because she didn't understand baseball but was
compelled to react to any kinetic in-game happening, guided
along my pre- and post-natal development with enough ef-
ficacy that I was not visibly damaged, baked grudgingly for
bake sales so I would not be the only one failing to contribute
to the bake sales. She had for most of my life been the only
person to love me.

I rolled down the window and she walked over. Her
eyes were red. Her tongue was split. The face changed into
something not human. She spoke words I somehow understood to be Sumerian.

"Nope, not her," I said to Monica.

78

After an hour of driving we saw a white cross and a sign
reading, "Food, Water, Respite from Anger," that seemed
promising as anything at that point.

We pulled in to a military style encampment, with
mess tents, personal tents, stores of dried goods, latrines,
and a dozen earnest-looking people busy performing one
survivalist task or another.

"Good day," shouted the apparent leader, "My name is
Jean Louis De Lebris De Gatineau."

"Hello Jean," I said, already having forgotten his hun-
dred or so odd names.

"You are welcome to stay here, but first, I look into
your eyes," said Jean L.D.L.D.G.

He looked into our eyes and deemed us unAngry, then gestured for a woman to bring us two metal cups of water. Something about those metal cups just screamed 'Frontier living.'

"Who is this guy?" Jean asked, indicating Bobo.

"That's Bobo," I said.

"So what's your deal?" asked Monica, skeptical after all the *folie a culte*, being in Chaos' dream, and the phony reptilian version of my mom.

Jean Louis De Lebris De Gatineau cleared his throat, and spoke, "We have united to fight for what is good. To fight for the future of the children. To fight for the world that God made and the Devil called Satan is in the process of destroying. To fight for a child to run with a stick and wave the stick like it was a sword while he is actually carrying a toy sword and he say, 'Now I have two swords...'" which must have been some specific memory of Jean's.

"Mmmkay..." said Monica.

"To oppose evil as man has opposed evil since the dawn of time. To oppose senseless violence and hate and live as God commanded in scripture. To keep kindness alive on earth. To pay h'omage to the feeling a poor young French Canadian boy feels when he sees the light of the sun shining through a bush onto a crooked path and realizes richness and material possessions mean nothing to a man with an eye for God's wonder. To shout, 'Do not worship Hopper lest you anger God in heaven.' To overcome the lust that has overwhelmed the people. To engage in man's simple pleasures like biting a peach..." at this he produced a peach from his tunic and took a theatrical bite, which he didn't have to do because I was already so sold.

"To exercise human compassion in the face of rot. To keep a respectful eye on the stars and heavens that were created by God. To sensibly use the glorious gift of language.

To fight using force if necessary, if evil confronts us. To never stand down in defence of…"

At this Jean Louis De Lebris De Gatineau was struck in the head by a bullet as a raiding party of twenty-five Bundsmen stormed the encampment, kicked down tents, shot some of the resistance, tied up the rest including Monica and me, began slicing faces, and of course knifing people's personal entry holes. Happily, Bobo ran at a great speed away from the Bund. I hoped he would find someone to take care of him.

When they got to me, I said, "Wait, I'm friends with Dan Good. Dan Good and I go back to when we were five years old."

The Bundsman sighed, got out his phone and texted someone.

"Tell him it's Lloyd MacDonald. Ask if he remembers the games of catch. Ask if he remembers the sleepovers."

"He's not interested," the Bundsmen said after a moment, which, believe it or not, hurt far worse than what was to come.

The Bundsman punctured the skin beneath my cheek bone and twisted in a perfect C-shape that removed my entire right cheek. That hurt like absolute hell, which is probably why I've been so blasé in describing all the other face-slicings up to this point in the narrative. The knife in my butt was no picnic either. Perhaps worse were the screams of Monica, who deserved the penetrations and peeling off of her face skin so much less than I did. Unlike the mercy Candy showed Scapino, we were left to bleed out, moaning in pain, moaning in woeful harmony with the newly faceless members of Jean Louis De Lebris De Gatineau's movement, until we ceased to be alive on earth. RIP Lloyd, Monica, members of Combray's movement.

79

Because Monica was roughly the same weight (136) as me (148) we bled out at approx. the same time, and consequently our disembodied souls spiraled towards oblivion in general proximity. Others who'd died at the Gatineau massacre were also spiraling towards oblivion, and occasionally one of these people would stop spiraling towards the light, having been sucked out of the oblivion spiral into a red gash in the oblivion spiral's (for want of better term) wall. I clung to Monica, assuming, not officially baptized as she was, she might be sucked into a red gash at any moment.

Fortunately, the two of us emerged out of the oblivion spiral into a place I perceived as looking like the Lac-Sainte Catherine Golf Course and Country Club. I say 'perceived' because Monica described it as looking to her like the gleaming retail mecca that is Toronto's The Eaton Centre.

A man at a fancy desk checked names against a gold-braided list. I recognized him as the actor Sterling Hayden, who had starred in *The Killing* and also *Dr. Strangelove*, which seemed to confirm once and for all that Stanley Kubrick was running the operation. When Monica approached him Sterling Hayden checked her name off and said, "Welcome to heaven."

"Thanks," she said.

I approached Sterling Hayden and said, "Loved you in *The Long Goodbye*. Please give my regards to Mr. Kubrick for his beautiful production of the end times."

"Afraid that won't be possible..." replied Sterling Hayden, "He was here, and did cast me in this role, but he recently departed."

"Where did he go?"

"Down below for…greater creative control."

"Does that mean Hopper and Scatman Crothers are also below? Scatman Crothers seemed like such a nice human being," I said.

"He secretly murdered three women," said Sterling Hayden.

"Oh."

"Name?"

"Lloyd MacDonald."

"Place of birth?"

"Lac-Sainte-Catherine, Ontario, Canada. POJ1M0."

"Not seeing you on this list. Nothing to be concerned about. Sometimes there are clerical errors," he said, and handed me a guest pass.

We greeted our respective loved ones, grandparents, second cousins, etc. Pierre ran up and licked our palms. I was heartened to see dogs weren't barred from heaven. My mom was nowhere in sight, meaning she was either still in the basement sipping from Mason jars or else roaming the desolate earth in demon form as recently depicted. I made small talk with Gary about heaven.

"So, how's heaven?" I asked.

"Pretty neat. You can do whatever you want. And everything is tailored to you individually. So say you and I sit down for a meal. For you it may seem like we are at an all-you-can-eat shrimp buffet, but for me it might be a fancy steakhouse. But we're both sitting in the same place, and there's never any discord, somehow," said Gary.

At this I went to an all-you-can-eat wing buffet and put a bunch of perfectly-sauced wings on a plate. "I'm eating wings," I said to Monica, "From an all-you-can-eat wing buffet."

"For me the buffet is providing fresh-tasting wraps like I had in Toronto once but could never find in L-S-C," she said.

Scapino approached the buffet.

"Hey Scapino," I said, "Sorry about slicing your face off."

"No big deal," he said, popping a piece of sushi into his mouth.

I played nine holes of golf with Bob Dylan. You're probably thinking, "Why would Bob Dylan want to play golf with crappy old Lloyd?" but again that's the subjective nature of heaven. Bob Dylan's personal soul consciousness was at that moment jamming with Blind Lemon Jefferson, but some aspect of Bob Dylan was playing golf with me. Incidentally, the manifestation of Bob Dylan playing golf with me cheated on almost every hole, which I found hilarious, being in heaven as we were.

After the golf game Blind Harv said hello, but I wasn't that interested so I left to chat with young Liz Taylor while Blind Harv continued talking to me in his subjective experience of heaven. I stroked subjective young Liz's black hair. I kissed her on the cheek. She didn't seem to mind. I was going to move in for an hj/br attempt, but figured with my guest pass I better not push it.

Then, although I had quit guitar after only a few months, I decided to jam with Bob Dylan and Blind Lemon Jefferson, so another subjective manifestation of those two was created to jam with me. I sang harmony with Bob on *Senor* and *Sign on the Cross* until a small crowd gathered and sat in astonishment at the raw power of our performance.

Monica and I walked through a field of cherry blossoms with her mother, whom I had never met in real life. My grandma and I played scrabble. I enjoyed a hot tub with busty 80s pop sensation Samantha Fox and Timothy. I discoursed briefly with Henry David Thoreau, and seemed to be right there with him, intellectually. I had a sixty-minute broadway wrestling match against Curt Hennig aka Mr. Perfect that awed an onlooking Nature Boy Buddy Rogers.

I was wishing I'd died much sooner when Sterling Hayden approached with a couple of heavies. Heavies for heaven anyway.

"Sir," said Sterling Hayden, "There's been a mistake."

80

"First, we'd like to establish our deep regret at this misunderstanding. You see, our sensors sometimes get confused when two new entrants to the afterlife are in contact with each other. Your clinging to Monica led to this error."

"You're about to tell me that Monica doesn't belong in heaven?" I asked.

Sterling Hayden laughed a little.

"No way. No fair. I tried to live a good life," I said.

"We have metrics, Mr. MacDonald. You see here during this period between your birth and right before the Anger you were on the cusp of entering heaven. We have a basic formula of service to others over service to self, and we want that to come out to at least .56. You were teetering right around .53 when the Anger began, but then the many murders and infidelities sent you down into the low 20s. Jeffrey Dahmer territory."

"But those were End Times, zombie-style killings," I said.

"Some were, yes, but the murder of J.P. Scalipi, for example, was completely unjustified. Also, the separated shoulder of Mert."

"Mert was a sports accident!" I shouted.

"Oh yes, that's right, I mean Burt. You maliciously jerked the wheel of the truck to separate Burt's shoulder."

"But he took advantage of those girls," I said.

"That brings up the infidelities. It's interesting to note that even with the murders you might have got in under probationary circumstances, but the wicked string of infidelities, often several per day, sent you plummeting downward."

"Damn those hussies!" I yelled, "What about Bob Dylan? He's here, and he cheated on Sara Dylan like a billion times."

"Bob Dylan brought a great deal of happiness to the world, whereas you did not do that," said Sterling Hayden.

"May I speak to God? May I ask God's forgiveness?" I asked.

"No, you may not. But here you'll find a rich irony. If at any point while on earth you'd have asked God's forgiveness you'd have seen an uptick in your numbers. One repentant prayer while at the Temagami Music Camp and you'd have gotten straight in."

"Your bedside manner leaves something to be desired," I said, "Not only are you casting me out of heaven, but you know you're really rubbing it in."

"It's your fault. You had free will. You acted poorly," said Sterling Hayden.

"So, since I was kind of on the cusp of heaven at one point anyway, can I be confident I'll be placed in purgatory, and can work my way back up after a few eons of boredom?"

"There is no purgatory," he said. "You will go to hell."

At this, a gaping red wound opened in the floor of Sterling Hayden's office.

"If you think I'm stepping into that hell wound you have another thing coming," I said.

Heavenly heavies got me by the arms and forced me into the gash.

"Wait," I said, "Can I at least say goodbye to my loved ones?"

"No sir. But you'll be seeing plenty of them where you're going," said Sterling Hayden, which I didn't understand at the time.

The last thing I saw in heaven was Alatragus Pino arriving with a new crop of souls.

"Oh come on," I screamed, only my nose and eyes still outside the hell wound, "He helped me slice Scapino's face."

"He also brought joy and mirth to the students of St. Michael's Collegiate by organizing dances and fundraisers in his bid for valedictorian," said Sterling Hayden.

"How can that possibly be releva…" I began, but didn't finish, because as of the 'va' sound I found myself in hell.

81

What really signified the beginning of End Times for me, back before hearing of the Bund, before Blind Harv's consumption, was the week of dreams that preceded the first news reports of worldwide Anger. Always the same identical dream.

I'm at the Sudbury International Film Festival, which I had attended each year since I was 14.50 due to the prohibitively high costs of the far-superior Toronto International Film Festival, and the fact that little outside the absolute broadest, mass-market, lowest-common-denominator films were ever screened in L-S-C's lone multiplex. To see any first-rate films in theatre it was Sudbury or nothing, which is pretty depressing if you know anything about Sudbury.

The screening I'm at sometimes changes. Sometimes it's a screening of *Anomalisa* and sometimes it's a screening of *The*

Forbidden Room, but the man is always the same. Seating is limited so I'm forced to sit beside a morbidly obese man covered in tumours. The tumours cascade downward from his face, bleeding a little, way worse than your standard fibromyalgia. He dabs at the bloody tumours with napkins, and has to hold up the tumours so they bleed less, or maybe just for comfort. His sides spill over his seat, occupying the plane of vertical space above my seat with bleeding tumour matter.

Anyway, that guy from the dreams was like my residence advisor in hell. I spent the first few million years in a stuffy little room with him, his boils bursting on me, him farting all the time, him saying inane things about film that I could not refute because he frequently cut out my tongue. The tongue would painfully grow back and then he'd cut it out again right before saying some really off-base thing about the work of Nicholas Roeg for example. Sometimes the Tumour Man and I would just hang out because given enough time and boredom anyone can develop a bond.

But the physical and psychological torture of my years with the Tumour Man was like a Swiss ski vacation compared with what would follow.

82

Some descriptive notes on hell: Hell time passes at roughly 84328 years per hour of earth time. There are clocks in hell, and I'm forced to monitor what's going on terrestrially, both in my dimension and others, that's how I provide so accurate a ratio. Hell would be a cakewalk without clocks.

After my internship period with the Tumour Man, I descended into my own hall of memories/dream-model of hell type-hell. My happiest moments screened ad nauseum on telepathic mind-screens I can't shut off. Hour after hour I watch Dan Good, Archambeault, and a bygone historic me laughing at a pizza party in the sixth grade, or scheming at a sleepover. That might not sound so torturous but it's the contrast that stings while solitary and unloved in the pit.

Worse are the alternate dimensions I'm forced to view. In some I go on living and am part of a weekly golf foursome with D.G., a clear-headed Lewis Orlovsky, and going home to hj/br combos with a Monica grown up to be beautiful. Better outcomes existed for my transdimensional proxies, but for whatever reason were blown by the Lloyd now rotting. This is the sadness. That's how I rot. Although *rot* is the wrong word because it conveys an eventual end. To rot, decompose, cease. There is no cessation.

Sometimes my mindscreens screen simply Pierre running beside me in a park. Then if I get lost in reverie the Tumour Man or someone like the Tumour Man comes in and stabs a huge blade through my kidneys and I writhe and moan knowing I will not die and my kidneys will eventually respawn.

The most painful worldline to observe features Monica and the chiseled boyfriend she goes on to marry playing ultimate Frisbee together, attending Jack Johnson concerts (lame!), buying properties, moving up in the world, swimming in hotel pools, having children, raising the children, taking the children to Ultimate Frisbee tournaments where the children watch from the sidelines, and I'm forced to watch that for a decade or two at a time, like the John Cusack character in *Being John Malkovich*.

There's unlimited access to Facebook in hell. Obviously I can't update my status, but only view statuses of peers,

and see them excel from perspective of pit, which is not altogether unlike the last several years of my earthly life.

There's no sleep in hell, but occasionally consciousness drifts into the equivalent of a dream = 'All a big misunderstanding' + 'I'm back on earth drinking a six pack and watching a compilation of sexploitation trailers on Netflix,' but then I 'wake up' and the Tumour Man has cut out my tongue and is using it as toilet paper and though cut out I still feel the sensations of his horrid anus where my tongue once was.

You never see the so-called Devil, Hitler, John Wayne or anyone exciting. I would describe my surroundings as a 4 x 8 concrete room, poorly ventilated, more boring than sinister. There's none of the burning depicted in literature. None of the molten lava depicted in cartoons. That would distract from the deeper and truer psychic pain of watching myself play golf with Dan Good in an alternate dimension where I didn't waste all my happiness and wind up in hell.

83

Now for the bad news. Having read this document to its conclusion, you, reader, will be among the first infected with Anger in what you consider 'the real world.' A cultural attaché, here, infernally, believed my story (visible to the attaché on my mindscreen) contained the right texture of bile needed for the cause. Not that I'm special. There are an infinite number of dimensions, and a near-infinite number of poison narratives being produced. The most corrosive appear in multiple dimensions. For example: the screenplay

and subsequent film of *Young Adult* appeared in nearly all dimensions because it is such a malefic shit in the face of human decency. I hope my story enjoys such a wide release.

How does it work? The poisoning is not based solely on my gross story, nor the dysfunction and cynicism celebrated in the *Young Adult* screenplay. When I turn in my manuscript, alpha-numeric codes will be embedded, of which I lack significant understanding, but it's basically a trio of Really Gross Narrative + Satanic Language Code + Numbers that has already done you in.

Why, would I, the unlikable yet generally half-decent narrator of this narrative contribute to something so destructive? I've got nothing against the world lines you've known and loved. I didn't have to invoke pestilential woe on the innocent populous of the multiverse. The attaché would have let me stay in my room.

Here's why: the worst part of hell is suffering unobserved, watching mindscreen Monica frolic through fields night and day, without the slightest possibility of incurring anyone's empathy. It is hardest to be sad when no one cares that you are sad.

Plus, privileges were bestowed upon me for composing a doom-portal type document. I got to consult with Francesca Woodman on cover art.

Firewalls were lifted so I could do Internet research. On Project Gutenberg I found these lines from *Heart of Darkness* to be a decent rationale for why I'd destroy your world to tell my story.

"I don't like work—no man does—but I like what is in the work—the chance to find yourself. Your own reality—for yourself not for others—what no other man can ever know. They can only see the mere show, and never can tell what it really means."

Maybe my show doesn't mean much, but the meaning of it meant much to me. I will never meet you, but now you know something of me. I apologize for damning you. I did warn you at the beginning, but you likely perceived that as puffery.

I'd hoped to be introduced to Hopper, Kubrick, or other luminaries orchestrating Anger diseases, but was not. However, there is talk of a wrap party after this round of [p] documents (as we refer to them) have been sent out.

One last little behind-the-scenes detail. How does a manuscript from hell get published in what you may consider the lone material universe? Easy, our publishing team dream-downloads the book into some writer or aspirant writer who believes the content original to him or her. Even these last explanatory sentences, hilariously enough. We infernal authors hope our efforts are dream-downloaded into someone with a big readership like Stephen King or at least the aptly named Diablo Cody. But, sometimes we have to settle for some hack who'll pathetically upload his year(s) of dream-downloaded effort onto Amazon and have it read by six relatives and a few disdainful peers, which is enough, given the intention.

Mike Sauve has written non-fiction for *The National Post*. His fiction has appeared in *McSweeney's*. His novel *The Wraith of Skrellman* was published by Montag Press. *The Apocalypse of Lloyd* is his second novel set in the dismal northern Ontario town of Lac-Sainte-Catherine.